Tricked

Tricked

A THIRD AND LAST TIME

Jack T. Reynolds

Library of Congress Control Number:		2014910378
ISBN:	Hardcover	978-1-4990-3413-4
	Softcover	978-1-4990-3414-1
	eBook	978-1-4990-3411-0

Unless otherwise indicated, all scripture quotations are from *The Holy Bible, English Standard Version® (ESV®)*. Copyright ©2001 by Crossway Bibles, a division of Good News Publishers. Used by permission. All rights reserved.

This book was printed in the United States of America.

Rev. date: 07/03/2014

To order additional copies of this book, contact:
Xlibris LLC
1-888-795-4274
www.Xlibris.com
Orders@Xlibris.com
633755

Contents

Dedication:

I dedicate this book to all of the women and children survivors that had to endure the disappointments and deceptions of those they trusted and were helplessly vulnerable to. They had their rights of happiness stripped away by abusive pretenders and in spite of the selfish webs of the abusers they still made it through... j.r.

Chapter One

JASON'S TURN

**"I HAVE NO PLEASURE IN DEATH FOR THE
WICKED, BUT THAT THE WICKED TURN FROM HIS
WAYS AND LIVE" GOD... Ez-33:11**

Jason proclaimed, "I'm often leery of my subliminal desire to
make vengeance my own, but when it comes to helpless children I
gladly become one with Oz. It's unexplainable how our spirits surge,
me as an ordinary man and Oz as what I hope is an angel. Somehow we
become one without me actually knowing or remembering anything
of it when the following morning comes. In some way, that I don't
quite understand, he goes out into the night and apparently wreaks
vengeance on child molesters. I'll tell you something honey, for some
reason I trust his cunning ability, not only to take over my body but
to enhance it with the extra ordinary physical strength and stamina
in order to pursue and inflict revenge upon those that have violated
the unwritten warnings of God concerning his children.

I guess I don't really have to tell you all of this because you're the
one that brings it to my attention when I come home late at night or
early the next morning all dirty and exhausted.

With Oz within me, I slightly remember being an out of control beast that is on a mission to aid children and to confront evil men. Kind of like, some kind of midnight super hero, that hunts down men that have been cursed enough to believe they can do as they please with the helpless. Some of those cursed idiots believe in mysterious powers that to them have proven to be mightier than all of the compassion instilled in the ordinary men. Or… maybe some men are much too helpless to resist the temptation. Sometimes I think maybe they're overwhelmed with perverted lust. Whatever the rationality may be; I'd like to see a continuing effort by those chosen good men and angels, if they truly exist, to put it to a stop without hesitation, without fear and without forgiveness. It's not just an eye for an eye. A child's life has no equal. One tear of a child should be a fair exchanged for the life of a predator, especially when it comes to sexual violence committed upon an innocent child, and to me, they are all innocent! They are here by the grace of God and the pride of His achievements. The very first commandment was 'To be fruitful and multiply,' not for sake of the lustful hunger of those that are obviously sick and evil!"

Helen: "Ok, Jason. Honey I'm just as angry as you are on the subject. I just keep wondering how you, or anybody for that matter, can get the message across, not only all over the city but the entire country. Child abuse is a very sick and selfish way to ruin someone's happiness forever. How are you going to even begin to do it?"

"Again I say, one by one or a thousand by a thousand!"

"Okay, just calm down a little. How about a little light heartedness on this starry night? You know something? It's been awhile since you've ventured out in the middle of the night honey; what's the matter Beyoncé doesn't like you anymore?"

"Ha-ha, that's funny. I wish it was Beyoncé; that would be a dream instead of a nightmare. She is one beautiful woman with those long pretty legs and…"

"Okay, never mind, that's enough!" Helen snapped, "I was only teasing you. I don't need to hear any more about your dream girl… I can always change the subject with you when I speak of Beyoncé or Haley…

Jason, on a more serious note; you know you have not gone out in the middle of the night and not come back until daylight in quite a while. In fact, as you know, there have been times that you didn't return for days. Do you think that maybe it's coming to an end or am I just dreaming that I won't have to worry about your safety anymore?"

"I'm sorry to say, because I know you worry; the last three nights have been filled with voices. I believe the voices were meant for Oz and for some unusual reason I was the one that received and understood them as pleas. The voices of seven children were crying as one voice. I believe my heart is turning cold and the anger of Oz is entering into my mind. I don't want you to worry any more than you have to. I will be as safe as I can if it comes to me consciously having to leave out and follow their directions on my own in the middle of the night. But, as you know my uncontrolled activity while I'm asleep is no stranger to either of us. My sub-conscious, or whatever you might want to call it when Oz has a mission to perform, doesn't exactly ask if it's alright to borrow my body," said Jason.

"It's you that I fear for. I know you are rational when it's just you. But, when your eyes blacken and you seem to be in some sort of trance that I can't bring you out of; I know that it's Oz. And then I am afraid for you, or your body, as you call it, you appear to be seven foot tall, every muscle in your body gets tense and solid. You seem to be aware of everything around you, but me, and each time I'm the only real person in the room. You move your head quickly from side to side as if something is suddenly drawing your attention to an oncoming runaway train. You ball up your fist dreadfully while sweat rolls from every inch of your body. You grunt loudly in anger and you often cry out in a frightening tone. I wish you were dreaming about Beyoncé", I wish… I wish.

Chapter Two

MESSAGES MEANT FOR OZ

That night as Jason slept, children's voices made their way into his dreams again even though they were intended for Oz they spoke loud and clear:

"Mr. Oz, please help us right now. I am the first; there are three now and soon to be seven. When his number is reached he will go the way of the locust and digest our souls, our dreams, and our last connection to God. Because we will never get to inhale a single breath of love from a mother, we will be forgotten in every aspect of existing. And then… he will return as he has seven times before and seven times before that, to start again to steal the lives of seven others. Please Mr. Oz, stop him now."

A second voice cried out louder than the first:

"I have been brought here to this incomplete place of worship, on this past night as number four; three others have been here longer than I and two are due to arrive at separate times from the place that we were rejected as worthy sacrifices. This will bring his count to six. He will bring one more as his seventh. We have all been rejected by the great one. Each time his servant ends our existence without a sacrifice to his god he himself gets stronger and older. His mate is our mother made of glass, she is known as fertility. She gives birth every eighty four months or every day. We are without names and are not attached by the flesh of a life cord.

Tonight we are here from near and not so far. The rain of this night will show you where we are. Follow your hunches and your instincts too and you will find our common place of birth. We have all been taken much too soon by the one that is known and is always trusted among you. He and others like him are the carriers of the curse. He has lived for many hundreds of years and is now known as a healer of sickness."

Jason was stirring and began to awaken from his deepest sleep;

"Wait! What do you want me to do? What rain, how can I find the rain? Where's the rain? Where are the children? Who is the evil man and where is he?"

"Honey wake up its 1:a.m., and you're mumbling in your sleep. You must be having a terrible nightmare."

"Okay, I'm alright... I've got to go back to sleep. Is it raining outside? I've got to get back to my dream and get some kind of direction. Please honey just let me sleep."

"Yes it is raining, how did you know? The weather man said no rain for the next few days, but someone needs to let him know that it's raining cats and dogs up here in the East Hills as we speak."

"Then I've got to get up now. I think it was a riddle and the rain is the key."

"Why, Jason? Why don't you get some rest here with me? Your gon'na have the Monday morning blues if you don't get some sleep. I'm sure that whatever it is it can wait til morning."

"No! The rain will show me where the children are Helen."

"What children? You won't be able to see your hands in front of your face. Look out there Jason you can't see the street lights from the patio door. The clouds are hanging lower than I've ever seen them and this will probably last all night. Please just relax and rest. I'll get you a warm glass of brandy that will chill you out."

"No, I've got to get up right now and find them. If the rain stops it will be too late and they may never be found."

"Find who Jason? Honey your scaring me. You're acting crazy again. Why can't you just let Oz find someone else to use for his crusade against rapist. Why is it always my man? I have a funny feeling about this sudden rain and you being called out instead of Oz. Please baby, don't leave me tonight. Why won't you answer me?"

Jason hurriedly dressed while Helen continued to plea to no avail. With Helen standing in the door behind him he ran down the short flight of steps and out into the night without hesitation. He got into his car and sat squeezing the steering wheel tightly without starting it.

"Please, just give me a sign, God give me something I can go on. I can't just drive out into the darkness and rely on blind luck."

He recalled that the child's voice mentioned an incomplete place of worship. He also recalled that less than a mile away there was a huge new church under construction and parts of it has sat abandoned for a few years.

"I wonder."

He sped off to the site and drove through a chain linked fence that was hung with a no trespassing sign blocking the way onto the property.

"Oh my God this is it. This is the place. I can feel it in my bones. It's so close to my home I wonder if I know the children. If it wasn't raining so hard I'd be able to see my complex across the highway."

He drove up into the field in front of the abandoned structure and onward up to a functioning church's parking lot where he parked. He stopped and stepped out of the car into the down pouring rain. Without hesitation he began to run towards the wooded area down over the nearby hill. The three story incomplete steel skeletal structure loomed to his right and quickly vanished in the night within minutes behind him as he ran past. Realizing that his visibility was less than twenty feet in every direction he slowed his run to a slow jog and then down to a cautious walk. He was constantly wiping the rain water from his face as he slowly descended deeper down into the wooded area. A quick flash of lightning revealed a lot of scattered debris all over the ground and seemingly under every young wild shrub. Again a flash of lightning lit up the night. This time he believed that he seen the shadow of a man behind some bushes about fifty feet forward in the direction he was going. The sight of a man's shadow in the darkness caused his hair to stand up on the back of his neck knowing that he was standing in an open field and very vulnerable with nothing to hide behind.

"Now what, I'm here in shear darkness, soaked to the bone. I may even be in the cross hairs of the bad guy's weapon. I'm in trouble. I need to stay calm and kick ass out here as a marine like I would anywhere else. Where in the hell are the children?"

He reached under his light hooded jacket and pulled out the one thing he had taken the time to bring along. It was his 9 mm pistol that he had named Bet-Lou when he was stationed over in Afghanistan. With her in his hand he felt a lot more secure considering the unknown factors of the darkness. A strong summer wind blew and added more confusion to the whereabouts of the origin of all the different sounds that were filling the stormy night. The wind made a roaring noise up in the tops of the small trees surrounding him. He suddenly paused and turned around 180 degrees while pointing Bet-Lou at everything that had the slightest movement out in his peripheral vision. Due to the fast pace of spine chilling events leading up to this point he was looking for something that resembled a possible bad guy that he could fire into. If it were not for his marine experience in combat, he probably would have shot at everything that moved, including the small bushes that swayed with the wind. He was suspicious of everything that he could not identify, and he reflected those suspicions by screaming out warnings and threats.

"I see you. Come on out and fight a grown man you child killing piece of shit," he shouted.

Nothing was there. He was over excited and kind of caught with his pants down completely out of position. He spat the rain water from his opened mouth while his eyes burned from the mixture of sweat and rain drops. His sockless shoes had filled with muddy water from a newly formed stream rushing down the hillside that he found himself standing in the middle of.

"Follow the stream," for reasons unknown to him he continued to blatantly talk loudly to himself and continuously waved his pistol around at the same time. He began taking big splashing steps as he continued to descend downward.

Another frightening flash of lighting, this time followed by the roaring roll of thunder, revealed what appeared to be a figure of a man holding his right arm out with a water soaked garment hanging on his fingertips. In Jason's mind that piece of clothing belonged to a slain child. After the delayed rumbling of another lightning bolt the night seemed to turn instantly much darker than it was before. He began to turn around and around trying to face every angle in an attempt to ward off anyone or anything that he may not be able to see approaching him in the darkness.

"Oh how I wish I had brought a flash light. Maybe my little led light on my keychain will help." He fumbled around and got the small light out of his hip pocket. He pushed the button on the rear of the four inch light and a quick beam of blue light projected just enough to see that the rain was unforgiving and coming down like there would be no end. With his small light leading the way he kept edging down the watery path. With-in a few more steps the light reflected what looked like a small child wrapped in plastic and floating near an old storm drain about six feet in front of him. Now he was a lot more than scared. With his adrenalin now pumping through his heart so loud that he could actually feel and hear it, he carelessly took another step and slipped down into the muddy basin with the floating object tumbling around him in about a foot of water. He kicked the bundle away from himself and pulled his upper body backwards up out onto the wet but solid surrounding land surface. He felt a warm tranquilizing feeling as he lay back facing the sky. He actually paused long enough to smile up at the clouded heavens in an attempt to keep himself calmed down enough to keep things in perspective without panicking again. He took a real deep comforting breath and wiped his brow. He realized that in his fall he had lost his flash light and pistol. The bundle of something bumped against his left leg and quickly brought him back to reality. Shocked by what he suspected, he tried to raise himself up into a sitting position, when a loud heavy voice broke the silence.

"Hold it right there!"

Jason laid there on his back with a bright flashlight shining into his face blinding him to everything but the barrel of a gun.

Chapter Three

FIGHTING AN ANGEL

Someone standing above his head beyond the pistol barrel kicked him hard in the right side of his rib cage, causing him to grunt in pain.

"It's over for you. What were you dumping here tonight, huh? What are you looking for?"

"I'm just out looking for rainbows, how about you," Jason answered.

"Oh you're a funny guy uh?"

He kicked Jason again this time in the back and twice as hard.

"How come you're not being funny now? Why are you here Mr. funny guy, where are the other three babies?" He asked, while administering another good hard kick.

"I told you, I'm looking for rainbows and baby killers, what about you?" Jason boldly answered.

This time Jason was ready for the kick and wrapped his arm around the man's leg below the knee and brought him down into the mud with him. As he hit the ground Jason found a little footing and with both hands grabbed the gun welding hand of his attacker. A loud bang and flash of light exploded inches from Jason left ear. With all of his weight and strength he laid himself across the man's right arm pinning it and his gun against the ground.

"You baby killing piece of shit. You'll never rape another," said Jason.

Jason had held tight to what turned out to be his own 9mm weapon and pulled his right arm away and attempted to place it against the man's head. In one quick motion the man slapped the weapon away and grabbed Jason by the back of his windbreaker and yanked him off of him and down onto the ground where he had just been thrown by Jason. Now the tables had been turned. Jason found himself helplessly struggling with a more than 250 pound beast that was now straddling his mid-section including both of his arms. The man shoved his pistol hard under Jason chin and spoke loud enough to shake the ground beneath them.

"Good–bye baby fucker," the voice said.

Lightning once more lit up the night this time it seemed to linger for minutes out of the darkness as Jason waited to hear the explosion that would end his life as he knew it.

Nothing… everything ceased as the man reached for the flashlight that lay within his reach. He shined the light directly into Jason's face and stood up without saying a word. Puzzled and not knowing what his next move should be Jason coughed a few times to buy some time and then he slowly lifted himself up half way out of the water and onto his elbow.

Chapter Four

SETTING A KILLER'S TRAP

"Why are you here Jason?"

Jason was puzzled, this time he had questions of his own.

"How do you know my name and more importantly, why didn't you shoot me? What's the matter you only kill babies," Jason boldly asked.

The unknown man ignored Jason, and asks another question.

"Where is Oz? You look like Oz but you're weak and bright eyed like a silly but brave human. Where is my angelic friend," he asked in his voice of thunder.

Again lightning flashed, briefly revealing the face of the man that had just for some strange reason spared his life. Jason recognized his friend, detective Ben, but he had the blackened eyes and huge muscles extruding from his face and neck like that of the angel Esha;

"Ben, is that you? What the fuck are you doing out here? I nearly had to whip your ass out here in this pouring down rain. Why didn't you identify yourself as a police officer?"

By now Jason had nearly made it up into a standing position and attempting not to slip again. But, as this night would have it with the ground being wet and slippery he lost his footing. He was still trying to balance himself to stay upright. The man he just referred to as

Ben held him strongly by the elbow preventing him from falling back down into the puddle of muddy water. He took one more close look at Jason; he then released his grip and headed off into the darkness of the night, leaving Jason and his, nowhere to be found 9mm down, in the basin.

Jason called out Ben's name while kicking around in the water trying to find his weapon, instead his right foot bumped against a tightly wrapped body of the small child that had been floating and tumbling around face down at the drain of the catch basin. He paused and took the time to feel the child's body to be sure that his ghastly find was real.

"Ben," he shouted, "Ben... oh shit, I've got to get out of here."

He realized that Ben had run off leaving him with the corpse of a child, without a flash light or a weapon to defend himself against whoever may have murdered the child and placed it at the basin.

He climbed, slipped and clawed his way up the water drenched hill side. After making it to the top he ran pass the vacant church and made his way back to his car that now sat next to an unmarked police car with someone asleep behind the wheel and the car door left wide open. Jason carefully maneuvered his way to the driver's side and recognized Ben with a somewhat deflated face that was half the size of that look-a-like beast down at the bottom of the path.

"Ben, wake up! This is no time to be sleeping, wake up man."

"Huh?"

"Wake up, there's something very strange going on here. I need you to get coherent very quickly. This is no bullshit, it seems that our body snatching angels have been called to this place and we've showed up instead."

Ben still groggy and unsure of his surrounding or where he was, looked at Jason with the whites of his eyes fully in place but blinking open and closed as if undecided if they were asleep or woke.

"Man I just had the strangest dream that I was about to capture a child killer single handedly. Jason, why are you standing out in the rain? Get into the car. I don't remember leaving my house to get here. How did you find me Jason?"

"Find you! You found me and just like one time before we got into a scuffle. Let me look into your eyes so I can be sure as to whom I'm talking to. Yup it's you. Big bloodshot eyes of brown instead of all black and your breath smells like somebody pissed in a fire. It's you all right."

"Don't be funny. I know it's me dummy. So… what in the hell are we doing here Bro."

"I don't really know. I also came out in this unpredicted rain to take on the same child killer as you. The difference is I'm wide awoke without the help of Oz and obviously not prepared. There is at least one dead child down at the bottom of that wooded hillside out there," he pointed. "I believe there may be more or at least another being brought here tonight."

"Holy shit! Are you serious? U'm gon'na call for some back-up and the swat team."

"No, no, wait Ben, he may have already left but I think he'll be coming back until he reaches his goals and goes into hiding for another seven years. If he sees the police activity he may dump the rest of the children someplace else and we will never catch him."

"Okay, you may have a point. Give me a moment to get my bearings and we'll get this motherfucker ourselves. How do you know all of this?"

"You may not believe me but I had the same dream you must have had, only Oz didn't show up to hear it and I did. So I guess now you or I have the strength of Oz or Esha. We're gon'na come up against a cunning child killer and whoever may be with him. I lost my gun down there somewhere down at the bottom of the path, thanks to you. The only good thing I can see now is that the rain is suddenly letting up."

"It's okay. I've got a shotgun and some other helpers in the trunk of the car and my 44 mag against my chest. I'm armed and ready to take this fucker in to jail my friend."

"Jail; wait Ben listen to me. Please don't think jail on this one. I know it's usually your way of thinking instead of mind but, let's just kill him before he kills us. Let's think like Oz and Esha, please. If we don't succeed in killing him tonight he will kill many more children somewhere else. Let's do exactly what they would do in this case. This man is a plaque headed for the destruction of the innocence in all children. We need to send the same message that he sends to God's children. The deference is we're good men hopefully being used as tools like Oz and Esha."

"Okay let's do it."

Chapter Five

WAITING FOR NUMBER SEVEN

The two men stood outside of the car in a moment of silence and then headed back down the path to kill a killer. It was 3:30 AM when they left the cars.

They waited patiently in the darkness until daylight was upon them without conversation and without fear. And finally Ben spoke;

"Well my brother, it seems he's not coming back."

"No, look over there," Jason pointed at what appeared to be the sudden presence of another child wrapped in bubble wrap and taped with duct tape under the nearby brush.

"It's a rolled up piece of carpet with more bubble wrap in the center of the roll and... I can see a pair of small feet through the plastic. That means he's been here and gone."

"What now?" Ben asked.

"According to my own dream he will bring his total to seven. There will be more before his mission is complete until the next killing in seven years. I don't think we should disturb the scene. I don't believe he will abandon his dump site until he gets them all here in one spot. According to the voices I heard in my dream; he will gather them here for a final ritual and move on to his next plan of worship."

"Yea Jason" Ben commented, "but what if there are already seven here?"

"In that case we've lost him, he won't return here during his abstention. Benjamin, he is coming back here with one more child. Don't ask me how I know this but I do. It may be just to make fools of you and me or should I say, Oz and Esha, or… maybe we can even throw in God Himself. Whatever his reason, believe what I say, he will be back."

"In that case let's search the area and see how many children are here, maybe he is not done or maybe he is, but either way I won't be finish until he is dead. I will find him, even if he… what did you call it, 'abstains'. Where ever he goes we'll find him."

"Now your talk'n like the Ben I know. Its daylight now, we should be able to find the poor babies. They don't seem to be really hidden, I would guess because no one comes in this area at all so his grave site is well chosen to give him the time he needs."

They walked together and found the two bodies that seemed to be the most recent. Then another two that appeared to have been there for at least a few days. With the two that had been wrapped in bubble wrap that made six. They searched high and low and just like Jason had suspected, the seventh child was yet to come and they would be ready and waiting when he returned.

"Hey what's wrong Jason, are you all right? You look as if you're going to pass-out or explode on me. I don't know which."

"No, I'm not alright. There are some very worried mother's that are missing their babies. They are all loved and adored. Now look at this site, all these poor children have been dumped here without compassion or care of who may be hurt forever. This beast and all like him should burn a thousand times before going into hell. And, on top of all of his evilness he has placed them in this field not a mile from where I live. He has put them in our lap and he's probably as happy as lark that he has completed exactly what he had set out to do. My comfort is in knowing that we're going to get him and he doesn't even suspect that we are on to him. I can't wait to kill him Benjamin, I can't wait until tonight."

"Just settle down a little. We'll get him this time. This may be the first time that his place for disposing of his victims has been discovered before his task was completed. I'm guessing that if there were others here, after last night's rain, the body or bodies would have washed down here to the catch basin. If this is where you and I scuffled last night, I have no Idea how he could have brought another of those last two without exposing himself to us."

"Maybe he had already left before we got back down here to set up our surveillance or maybe he just doesn't give a shit that we may be on to him, either way if you are right he has one more time to try and trick us again."

Chapter Six

WHO IS THE BAD GUY?

"Well you're right, about there being only six Jason. I wonder how anyone could do this kind of shit and go about their life as if they've done nothing wrong. We may have had a friendly conversation with him somewhere along the line. He may be our doctor or our banker or the man at the corner store. In fact, what about that guy down in Homewood that has the candy store, you know he is known to have molested a few children. Maybe he has graduated to wanting them dead so they cannot talk or something."

"No Benjamin, I have a feeling this one has a deferent kind of access to children. Something like an orphanage or some organization, a church that would allow enough time to pass without a real search for the missing children until it's too late. There has to be more to it than an ordinary man."

"This must be the first time he's struck in the east side of Pittsburgh or the Wilkinsburg area. I faintly recall hearing of at least three times that bodies of children have been discovered in groups in other places."

"In my dream one of the voices referred to him as being like a locust. I'm guessing that may mean that he strikes and resumes his normal life for another seven years. For some reason I believe it's some sort of spiritual ritual that he does again and again."

"When I get back to the office I'll have my girl run a check on missing children and see if there have been any serial killings that would substantiate your theory."

After another hour of searching without finding that seventh body Ben concluded.

"Let's get here tonight before dark and catch him in the act. I won't get the force involved yet because you are right, he would be spooked and we'll have a harder time finding him once he leaves this area."

"And you know the news media would be all over the place, and guess what; we won't get the bad guy."

Later that day after re-acquainting himself to Helen and getting some much needed sleep; Helen allowed an urgent call from detective Ben to come through.

"Hey my brother," he started. "I hope you got some rest. My girl at the office checked every source available to us on line. There have only been three missing children reports in the tri-state area in the six to ten year old range. Two of the kids were found it turned out that they were part of a domestic custody issues and the other was found to have fallen in and old dried up well and declared an accidental death."

"That means one of two things; that they've come from afar or from an institution where a missing child wouldn't be missed by family members. I recall that the voice in my dream stated that, 'they had come from near not far'. I believe that she was eliminating the need to expand our search to places far away. I'm going to call you back in a few; I have something I want to check on."

Jason spoke to Ben several times during the morning while he was in front of his laptop reading the national news dated back as far as fifty years trying to track down the records of the locust type predators. One day he called Ben and informed him that he had found a woman that he believed could dig up articles in most major cities from Dallas Texas to New York to Los Angelis and Chicago. He told Jason that he was going to give her a couple 'a bucks to see what she could come up with involving missing children and bodies found in mass graves. He was hoping to find a pattern that may lead to the where a-bouts of not only the locust killer but any other monster that may be out there.

Jason knew that the locust killer had to be working out of Pittsburgh area but he was thinking that the killer had enough time in that seven year period to be able to travel and snatch children from other places. He also gave some thought to how he could search locally and locate grave sites that may have never been found. He decided that it would be too time consuming and he wouldn't know where to start. His main concern was to find where the children were taken from.

Jason went on line in search of children missing over the last twenty one years. He was seeking a pattern of information that may indicate seven or so missing children in a short period of time and in close geographical proximity. And... perhaps narrowing it down the ages closer to seven years old. He had a hunch.

In the information gathered there was no pattern of missing children in the Western Pennsylvania area that stood out as obvious; however there had been a distinct pattern of children found in grave-like crime scenes. The pattern seemed to be; groups of six or seven. There was one in Erie Pennsylvania, Youngstown Ohio, and Deep Creek Maryland, a similar one in Wheeling West Virginia and also Uniontown Pennsylvania, about seven years ago. Jason called Ben and shared his findings.

"Hey Benjamin, listen to this. There has not been a pattern of missing children reported that fits what we are looking for. But get this, there has been a pattern over more than forty years of make shift grave sites that were found with young children between the ages of five and eight, all right here within seventy miles from Pittsburgh. It seems that the most recent was down in Uniontown where someone discovered seven decomposed bodies just off of route forty while looking for civil war artifacts. In two thousand five they found six children corpse that hadn't been buried long, up where they were digging on the Erie beach project. This kind of grave site crime scene seems to have been going on as far back as the media has covered these kinds of cases. That may explain why my dream voice made reference to her murderer as the locust killer. I'm hoping that you and I can catch him tonight with his seventh victim and bring his or their reign of terror to a tragic end before he goes into hiding.

"I guess there is a pretty good chance that his seventh victim, in this case, is already dead making it impossible for us to try and rescue him or her."

"I would agree. I'll tell you what. I'll meet you in back of the church just before dark. With a little luck we may be able to surprise him and take him down forever. Do you think we should get more men involved or take him on by ourselves?"

"No, no, Jason… I agree with what you said before, he may sense something and dump the child someplace else and we'd have a much harder time finding who you have dubbed as the locust killer."

9/11/13 at 8:03 pm

When Jason arrived Ben had been there waiting for more than thirty minutes. It was just beginning to get dark. Unlike last night the sky was clear and the temperature was warm. Jason assumed that he was prepared this time for anything or body that may cross his path. He had a strong flashlight and his fully loaded pistol named Bet-Lou with an extra three clips that he intended to unload into the locust.

As they briskly walked side by side down towards the catch basin they calmly talked about the good old days out at the South Park swimming pool to ease the tension. When they were teenagers that's where they went every Sunday afternoon to find girls from the city.

"Man, those were the good ole days," said Ben, "back when I had more broads than you or anybody else from Coverdale."

"Now that's bullshit at its best. You ain't never had more girlfriends than I had, so stop talk'n that jive."

The closer they got the lower their voices became, until they were finally silent with guns in hand. Ben whispered;

"Be careful Jason, we both know how strong an evil man can be. I don't believe that it was a coincidence that this place is so close to your home and in my precinct was accidently chosen as a grave site. This could be about Oz and Esha and a trap to destroy them."

"Back-at-cha, Benjamin. I know this is not a game so let's stay close together and get out of here as quickly as possible." Jason lightened up the whispering words by adding to the conversation about being in a hurry to get back to Helen; 'she was waiting for him in an outfit that she takes her showers in at the end of each day.'

"Outfit, nobody showers with cloths on."

"That's my point brother."

"Um-m-m, now I know what you're talking about. I can see that cute little outfit in my mind as we speak..."

"Watch it now, just watch what you're thinking there buddy."

"Yea, well you brought it up bro, I just commented," Ben said as he swatted Jason shoulder and chuckled a little.

They slowed their pace again as they were about to reach the target area at about fifty yards away.

Ben had confidence that his many years of police experience and his two hundred and fifty pound body of weight lifting muscles, would bring him and Jason through this without a scratch, not to mention his 44 caliber weapon and of course Jason's courage and x-marine skills. As quiet as it's kept, Jason was not always just a good hearted soft spoken building contractor. Before his civilian life as a business man and settling down with his side kick, Helen, he was a hell raiser in his own ranks. He was a U.S. Marine not just an ordinary marine, he was a marksman that was ordered to and succeeded at taking down more than thirty enemy terrorist. That's a kill ratio higher than any other documented during the start of Afghanistan conflict.

8:35 p.m.

"It's just as we left it. It's starting to smell terrible down here even through the taped bubble-rap."

"Let's get ready for our friend."

The time passed slowly without any sign of the locust. A couple of raccoons that had somehow found their way into the city had to be quietly shooed away, but other than that, everything was at a standstill.

12:15 a.m.

"Listen," Ben whispered, "I think we're finally getting some company."

They both listened closely and focused on the sound of something being dragged up the hill through the brush from just below the catch basin.

"Get ready Jason I think our man has arrived right on time."

"I'm as ready as I'll ever be."

They could barely make out a silhouette of a man dragging a piece of rolled carpet behind him heading right for the basin.

"Not yet..." Ben whispered, "not yet, let him get all the way to the basin.

Okay let's get his ass now!"

They both jumped out of hiding and surprised the man. He started shouting, dropped his bundle and started to run back down the hill. Jason took a few leaping steps and tackled him to the ground, where Ben quickly caught up and placed his size twelve foot upon his neck just below his chin and placed his gun against the man's mouth. The man was attempting to scream that he hadn't done anything.

"Wait, wait please I didn't do anything wrong. Please don't shoot me," he said with a muffled voice that Ben or Jason could hardly make out because of Ben's foot being pressed upon his face.

Jason had gotten up and was shining the flash light into the face of a man while placing his own foot upon the man's chest and his gun also pointed down at the man's head ready to fire.

"I'm not the one you want, you've been tricked," the man shouted.

"Shut up! Keep your hands out where we can see them."

Ben cuffed him and pulled him up into a sitting position.

"Okay sir I'll do anything you say, just don't shoot me."

"What have you got in that rolled up piece of carpet," Ben asked while Jason was already unrolling it to discover that it was empty.

"I don't know" the man said. "I was paid by a tall blond haired white man to bring it up here to someone named Oz, with a message."

Jason finished un-rolling what he had thought was carpet instead it was an old rolled up painter's tarp filled with trash bags and trash.

Ben roughly dragged the man over to a nearby tree and used another pair of cuffs to cuff him more securely.

"Trash, nothing but trash," Jason repeated.

Under the beam of his flashlight all he could make out was painter's rags and paper trash. He turned to the man, held his flashlight and his gun to his head and shouted;

"Speak up or I'll blow your fuck'n head off!"

The man appeared to be about thirty five years old and not more than about one hundred and thirty pounds in weight. He smelled like rotten Mogen David wine mixed with the pungent smell of street level marijuana. He was dressed in a filthy ragged auto mechanic zip-up jumpsuit.

"Where's the message?"

"No, no, no, he didn't give me a note, he just told me what to say. He paid me to tell someone named Oz and Esha or some name like that."

"Tell them what," asked Ben.

"He said the kid is in your car behind the church. And then he said to tell you he'll see you in about seven years with some more rejected sacrifices. That's what he said; I swear to you, I had never seen him before in my life. Look in my pocket there's a hundred dollar bill. You can have it but please don't shoot me"

Chapter Seven

TRICKED ONCE

"Say to the Israelites, if the community closes their eyes when a man sacrifices one of his children to Molech and if they fail to put him to death, I myself will set my face against him and his family and will cut them off from their people together with all who follow him into prostituting themselves to Molech" GOD; Leviticus 20:2-5

Ben and Jason looked at each other under the light projected by the flashlight still shining in the drunken man's face.

"Leave him here he can't get loose from the cuffs. We had better get back up there and check out his story. You had better be telling the truth," Ben said as he re-directed his attention to the cuffed man, "or I'm going to come back down here and put you out of your misery."

They started their long climb back up the hill heading for their own cars based upon the message that the drunken man had given them. They were dam near running up the hillside, puffing hard while talking as they went; Jason blurted out a question.

"So, what do you make of our new development? Do you think

this asshole is playing us for some reason or do you think this is all a coincidence?"

"I don't know Jason. If he is, he surely has taken me over my limit of toleration. Right now I'm just boiling with anger and walking this hillside is whipping my ass. Anyway, we'll know in a few minutes won't we?"

Suddenly the loud sounds of multiple sirens filled the air. The local volunteer fire station was less than a mile from where they were and the warning siren was sitting just on top of the next hill near East Hills Shopping Center.

Up ahead the sky above was lit up bright orange to the point that they could see the black billowing smoke and flying ashes as if they were standing near the source of the fire. They both had a hunch what was burning. They had stepped up the pace to a complete run when they suddenly heard two shots fired in succession down the hill behind them.

Now the whole hillside seemed to be screaming with the noise of sirens, horns blowing and the echoes of the gun shots. Both Ben and Jason were confused as to which way to go; down where the gun shots were fired or up to what they assumed would be their own burning cars. Either way, they instantly knew that this personal attempt to capture a killer had backfired and was now going to be on every news channel in the city of Pittsburgh.

Filled with obvious indecision they looked directly at each other and turned back around. They wanted their killer.

"Shit Jason, we've been played like a fiddle at a Tennessee the opera!"

They ran back down towards the basin as fast as they possibly could without tumbling down the hillside.

With guns and flashlights in hand they reached the basin in just a few minutes. Jason got there a little ahead of Ben who was just a few steps behind. They both leveled their lights on the cuffed man. He had been shot twice in the face with what must have been a 45calibor weapon.

"Careful Jason this may be a trap!"

Ben slowed the approach and short circled around the area looking for the shooter. When he finally walked up to the cuffed man he found that he had a note stuck under his collar. It read;

'Sorry I couldn't invite you and Oz to the party this time. I would have liked to send you both off to hell with this gentleman. It would

have been my pleasure. None the less, thank you both for the brief excitement. Maybe I'll see you all in seven."

They were both bewildered and stood there momentarily stunned with their heads hung and their hands down at their sides.

"Come on Benjamin, well the shit is going to hit the fan now, let's pull out of this stand still and get back up to the top."

By the time they reached their burning cars the actual flames had been put out. Ben identified himself as a police officer and instructed the firemen to call homicide to the scene. Just then, one of the firemen walked up and informed the fire chief that there was a child's body inside of one of the burnt out cars.

He said, 'he or she had been bound and gagged and left in the back seat.'

Ben and Jason sat down on the steps of the fire truck dazed, saddened and furious as they glanced at each other and hung their sights on the burnt out vehicles.

"I guess you could say we fucked up, uh Jason?"

"Yea... I guess you could say that. And you could also say that, I'm not happy with the way we have been played by this... whatever he is. I wonder if Oz and Esha would have handled it smarter and maybe saved that seventh child or at least the drunken man's life. Or would they have fallen for the same trickery? Maybe Helen was right. Maybe I, being just the man named Jason, should have left the roll of a hero up to Oz."

"I don't know about that," Ben said with a stern and angry look on his face, "but I do know that nothing, as the old saying goes, is over until the fat lady sings. In other words, this is just part one and not the final curtain. Right now we are the fools of his evil escapades, but I pledge to you, I'm going to get this fucker if it takes the rest of my days"

With-in fifteen minutes from the time the firemen put out the fire, the county police and all of the Pittsburgh news media was on scene of the burnt out cars and down at the catch basin where the dead man lays. It was going to take quite a while for the law officials to properly secure the area and recover the bodies that Jason and Ben had to leave behind.

"Well Jason there's nothing else we can do here tonight. I've asked one of the officers to drop you off at home. Call me tomorrow if you would like to hang around with me during the site investigation. I'm sure there will be a lot of un-answered questions once the crime team gets here and does what they do. The lab people will follow up and hopefully be able to shed some additional light on times, causes and methods of death. In the mean time you need to get some rest. I know you're pissed off and hurt just as I am Bro. I just want you to know that no one could have put forth a better effort than we did under the circumstances. Again I say, our locust killer has won the first round but we're gon'na get'm; I'm say'n, you and I not Oz and Esha. Just you and I, okay?"

"Yea Benjamin, I'm with you on that and your right, I do need to get a little rest and think this thing through before it drives me crazy with hate. We won't be tricked again if we ever get another chance that I guarantee. I don't want to have to wait for him to reappear, I want to track him down and just have the pleasure of piss'n on his body."

Jason took one more look over at the burned cars and then back at Ben.

"Please keep me updated and don't make a real move without me. I believe I have an idea on how to trick him out of hiding."

"For sure brother, you can count on it."

They pulled each other close with clasped hands against the chest in soulful fashion and parted ways.

Chapter Eight

BODY COUNT

**"God hates the hands that shed
the blood of the innocent"**

Three days later Ben called Jason with an update.

"Jason my friend here's the deal. There were eight bodies recovered including the messenger. The autopsies revealed quite a surprise, but I think you may be ahead of them on the motives with your locust killer theory.

Two of those kids; by the way... their ages from what I was told, were very hard to pin point. They were all believed to be about seven years old but they were all extremely under developed for their age. Anyway, as I was saying, two of the children one boy one girl, died of strangulation. Three more; a boy and two girls', died of some sort of affixation. The final two, also a boy and girl, were burned beyond recognition, seemingly an act of torcher. One of those final two was the one found inside of my car. All but one seems to have been violently sexually molested at some point and time, before and after their death. Two of girls were sexually violated to the extreme. They were bound together like mummies from head to foot and apparently died while in bondage. Strangely enough, one of the victims appears to have been dead for more than a month. The final victim, again, the one found in my car, seems to have been tortured with some kind of iron poker even before being set on fire in the car. He's believed to have been murdered over the last twenty four hours; a second possibility of his cause of death may have been shock.

There is an even more puzzling part to all of this aside from the fact that they were all killed elsewhere. Three of the children were of African American decent, two were Oriental and two were Hispanic. And there was something else that caught my eye, bear with me for a moment, I'm looking through the paper work, oh yea… here it goes, it says three of the bodies have the name Molech branded into the skin of their stomach and all three appear to have been tortured in the same way. You know Jason I personally believe there was some kind of racial issue pertaining to how and who was put to death. This could be racial or the work of a religious cult but I don't think most religious cults care what color their victims are; do they?"

"That's a good question that I can't answer. I would think that race would not be an issue but I do know that gods that demanded sacrifices certainly preferred one type of sacrifice over another; even our own God had preferences. So, apparently what and who was sacrificed had some kind of meaning.

Based on what you've just said to me it seems that there is a lot more to these killings than meets the eyes. Everything just keeps on getting more and more disturbing to heartfelt feelings. I hope we can get to the roots of this by getting to every person that has become involved, even if they believe themselves as god. Today I'm going to read up on what it may take to kill or destroy one god or another. As ridicules as it seems, there are many people that believe in gods, even if they know that there is a cruel sickness involved in what they have decided to worship. You would think that no matter what is written in bibles or tabloids, that they would at least attempt to reason that some things are lies and deceptions used to gain selfish glory and the praise of fools.

I'm very distraught Benjamin, you might even call how I feel right at this moment depressed, but above all I'm pissed off. Right now I wish there was a way for me to summon Oz and unleash him on a rampage to destroy all harmful graven images in addition to the lives and souls of men that have taken it upon themselves to become self-claimed gods at the expense of someone else's right to live. I'm angry and I just want to retaliate, right now!"

"You know I say again… if you would like to come with me tomorrow morning for one more look your welcome."

"At this point I pass Benjamin. I have a feeling that the site there is only a dumping ground. But you know I want to help you track him down. Those children were obviously abused and sacrifice. This may be bigger than the both of us. Helen said that I'm not allowed to play with you anymore as Jason. She wants me to wait for Oz. She thinks that our counter parts are more capable of handling these types of un-godly predators and that we, should stick to being family men or fishermen. To put it a better way, she's just simply afraid for us."

"Yea, and you know what Bro… she may very well be right. But, that doesn't mean that they can do anything without you and me. You and Oz are one of the same just like Esha and I. When we are spiritually connected we are inseparable to say the least. As you know you and I are very protective Alfa type males. We'll succeed at what we take on or die trying. Maybe that's why Oz and Esha chose us."

"As Helen often says to me when I'm attempting to explain; that was well put Benjamin, so let's give our best shot to do him in or die trying."

Chapter Nine

Helen: "Honey, why do you suppose so many men physically harm women and children these days?"

"I don't know. I do know that there should be a special place for them deep down deep in the cells of hell. I recently read that some writer has semi-concluded that the desire to beat and rape women and children is a curse that has transcended for hundreds of years. The notion that men can find themselves hopeless against an inner lust or desire to rape women or to be sexual with a young child is frightening and yet this theory presented by Jackson Thomas may have some merit."

"It really sounds more like a search for excuses. Maybe even a little too much of trying to find reason or rhyme for an act that should only be accepted as a cruel sin and should be punished by death at first thought," said Helen.

"Yea, I agree but let me read to you what he has gathered based upon what he calls logic when every other explanation falls short of possibility.

He says, 'Young women and children have been the targets of some of the most powerful men in history as well as the common man of the fields.' He also says; 'there was biblical indication that a god by the name of Molech preferred children be sacrificed in place of animals or other sacrifices made to the God of Abraham.' I used to wonder why virgins were thought to be the best to be thrown to the gods. That would certainly explain why they may have continued to get younger if they suspected that they may be thrown off of a cliff or into a fire. The last thing you would want to be is a virgin in that case; thus 'the god made him do it' or the devil whichever he preferred, was the ultimate spiritual guidance towards sex with children.

'It would be viewed as a blessing of leisure,' he wrote that 'men longed to be as gods especially when the man is of hierarchy and all that he has cannot be enough. As part of a curse, man hungers for conquest of other men knowing that God himself has given men that blessing and reward, or more so, as punishment for those who have violated an instruction or command.' This man stated that 'there were rituals perform by men having anal sex with other men that had so-called sinned, and it was being recognized as an acceptable sacrificial act to certain gods for forgiveness.'"

"It seems to me it went something like, you sinned so if I do you in the butt as a demeaning punishment, you will be punished enough and forgiven," said Helen. "Maybe that's where the notion of being gay started. Maybe those that performed the male part of the act found the power of sexual domination over another man to be as gratifying as their domination over a young woman, only without the threat adultery or the chance of unwanted children. And those that continued to make the sacrifice willingly somehow found it pleasurable enough to identify it, or misinterpret it, as an act of a possible third gender, sound dumb to me, but men have been known think and to do the strangest things when given idle time. It stands to reason that to own or have total control over someone or a whole race of people that themselves believe they have been cursed by God and that they deserve to be abused as part of their punishment without mercy means they are blessed even if the hunger goes beyond the spiritual commandments. Abusers may think that all those below them in social status are cursed, meaning in essence, God doesn't approve of something they or their fathers have done or didn't do; so they are destined to serve. They are at the disposal of the stronger or strongest of men to do as they please. What could be more desirable than to be as a god, beyond reproach and have the power to determine what is right or wrong based upon the fact that you have chosen it to be. Even if you know that it's wrong you have made it right in your own mind. And even more so, what can be more meaningful to a person that believes he or she is cursed and living up to the expectations of God by submitting to the punishment that your fathers rightfully deserve and you must pay to win God's forgiveness."

"Wow, you're really up to par on your reasoning today and I totally agree with you on every word of it.

Anyway," said Jason "he goes on to say,

'A pedophile has chosen to perform a sexual act against a child, while doing so he has convinced himself that it is an acceptable thing to do because of who he or she has become. Their worthiness of being able to dominate or abuse someone else within their own circle of life is warranted and the blame can easily be placed upon an uncontrollable lust that is instilled by his own natural hunger for sex. The passionate need to perform sex without being fruitful is overwhelming for the evil spirit in mankind. In that moment a child's life has no meaning other than to satisfy his own personal desire to reach the godly pleasure of an orgasm.

As for my own thoughts on the matter; in these days it doesn't always seem to be about power or being god like. In a lot of cases it's just plain old perverted lust brought on by a sex driven society that often allows these acts to be justified by the abuse of drugs or alcohol or the notion that a child can be tempting and promiscuous just by being present and innocent. You throw those things in together with opportunity and plain old stupidity and you come up with a pedophile and the type of man that only a mother could love once he is exposed. It can get quite complicated and at times acceptable when the rapist is a loved family member that believes that he can get away with it through denial; even if he is suspected or caught red handed in the act.

In some cases that I know of, the lust of the rapist is so strong that he doesn't think of or care whether he may be caught while he is in the act of committing rape. His or her fear becomes a reality after satisfaction is reached and realization sets in that he may be caught and embarrassed or be punished or go to prison forever. Then and only then do they become afraid and sorry for the act that they've committed. After the threat of being exposed passes and they appear to have gotten away with the crime they just wait until they get another erection and an opportunity to satisfy that same lust again. For this kind of molester it has nothing to do with an inferior person being cursed because of a slave like possession. It's just a plain and simple evil that needs to always have consequences that fit the devastating crime regardless to the age of the predator it must be dealt with.

Furthermore, I personally think that even if a god chooses to harm a child or any of those that are harmless or helpless, he or she should face the consequences of being cut down by those of us that believe we are chosen to protect the innocence by whatever means necessary. That's what I think without a doubt. I believe a man should know where to draw the line. In this case every human has the right to the comforts provided by nature, peace and good will. I would take down a king or a god or an ordinary man for the so called blessing of knowing that every life is sacred and worth fighting to preserve. So… be it right or wrong, I would put my life on the line to protect my children, yours or anyone else's against something that may call itself a man or a god."

"Wow, I'm impressed. So who is cursed do you suppose? Is it the predator or the prey in these cases?"

"Well, he says, it's the predator and I agree but a curse is only a curse when the consequences are executed by those that won't stand for the wrongful mistreatment of a child," said Jason.

"Well said, but tell me how can just little' olé you and your nine comrade stand up against such an evil army of well-adjusted sexual predators that believe that what they do they have a right to do based upon their god-like superiority?"

"One way is that we will have no pity. These cursed sectors of society are truly cowards that hide behind denial and secrecy. One by one or a thousand by a thousand we will hunt them down and send them to their maker. They are not superior to anything other than their own god some time known as Satin, and even he may be better than they in some ways.

"Jason, how will you know if they are guilty of such heinous crimes without a trial? How can you take the law into your own hands without having some doubt as to their guilt or innocence?"

"That's the easy part. Just as they are cursed with the yearning to control the minds and bodies of children and to destroy their spiritual peace, we are blessed to know the look, smell and reactions of a child pedophile as well. They want to be a god; the royal pedophiles, starting with religious pretenders and down to those that rape their own children, whether they are poor, rich or as wealthy as a king, we won't ever hunger to misjudge or harm the innocent but we will exist only to stand in the way of their ruthlessness and selfish intent."

"Again, I'm impressed by an answer that I already knew. What about the many nights that you are overcome with the helplessness to yield to Oz.

Is he as compassionate as you when it comes to caring or is he simply non-forgiving?"

Chapter Ten

Three weeks later.......

The news media's questions and answers saga had wined down across the city. The neighborhood had its ongoing crimes led by empty headed drug abusers, domestic violence and day to day gossip to contend with. The notion that people prefer justice only applies to those seeking justice for themselves. Un-wanted children have no recourse. They often take the blunt of abuse, live un-loved and learn to exist up through adulthood under a constant bombardment of instructions and rules without compassion. Un-wanted children aren't always parentless. In these days of heavy drug use and a popular move among young mothers to disregard warnings and indulge in self-satisfaction; children have quite often become victims of neglect. Often times it is a job or an education schedule that determines the success of a young mother. A most dangerous circumstance is the desperate mother that finds a male to be her lover and her baby sitter and gives him responsibilities all in one.

Often times un-attended and un-wanted children are targets of predatory idle handed men and the organized child sex rings. Opportunity is what all predators keep themselves aware of. Some create the opportunity, some wait for it and others purchase it with money or trade it for drugs. Jason and the ten good men are rare. They are offended by the need of a predator to disregard every aspect of decency to satisfy their own guest and thoughtlessness to ruin the lives of children as a lifelong pedophile.

Chapter Eleven

Ben had gone to the crime site nearly every day looking for something that may have been overlooked.

One Saturday morning it was Jason that was feeling the need to go to the site based upon something that he vaguely remembered in one of his recent dreams. Jason called and convinced Ben to take one last look with him.

Ben agreed and met Jason behind the abandoned steel structure not far from the upper entrance where their cars were burned and the tragedy took place. He drove up on his especially built Harley looking more like one of hell's angels rather than a police detective.

When the roaring bike motor was finally turned off he pulled down his sun glasses and questioned Jason with the cool look of an East Coast biker.

"So, Mr. Jason... what is it that we are looking for that hasn't already been found? Do you have any idea as to what brought this urge on for you to come out here after all this time?"

Just then and before Jason could answered about fifty other bikers pulled up causing the whole hillside to vibrate to the roaring of their high powered up engines.

"What's all this Benjamin?"

"I thought you may need the help of some real men of courage that are volunteers from the bike club that I belong to."

"Well to search every inch from the top to the bottom of the hillside we can use all the help we can get. And who would do that better than, 'real men of courage.'

To answer your question; no, I don't know why I felt the need to take one more look. It makes me sick to have to see this place again, but something keeps telling me that the urge wouldn't be inside of me so strongly if there wasn't a reason."

"Believe me I understand. I've had that same urge every day since the day that it happened. I've walked this area a hundred times back and forth without anything changing but my attitude."

"Well let's get started."

Ben instructed his volunteers to walk shoulder to shoulder and to look for anything that may appear to be out of the ordinary

Ben and Jason went directly down over the hill and walked around the catch basin in every direction while other bikers walk heads down over the entire area. They went over the whole hillside inch by inch for more than three long hours without finding any additional clues.

"Well Benjamin I guess it's time to thank your men and admit that there is nothing here that can be helpful. I don't know about you but I'm getting hungry. How-bout we go down to Simmie's restaurant over on Frankstown and get a fish sandwich for everybody, I'll buy."

"That sounds like a winner to me bro. You know I really don't know why I keep feeling like we've missed something, I guess it's because the case is becoming cold and I'm afraid he may have slipped away to live and do it again. I'm just sick about it. You're always pretty lucky when it comes to sensing things and I was hoping he had dropped a name tag or his cell phone. I don't know what, but anything to get me closer to his trail."

"I'm sorry Benjamin. I feel the same way you do. I keep having split second flashes in my dreams, that he dropped a photograph of himself. Now that really makes no sense but I don't know, it always seems like a message meant for Oz that I'm not quite getting. I guess we've just got to wait for something more substantial."… Jason hadn't quite finish when his phone rang, it was Helen.

"Hey baby what's up? Ben and I and a whole heap of friends are about to run up to Simmie's for a fish sandwich, do you want to meet us there?"

Helen told Jason that she was already parked up behind where he had told her that the crimes took place. She said there were about a thousand Harleys in the front lot so she park closer to the playground side of the church where she thought she would find him and Ben.

"I don't remember seeing a playground but you just stay right there. We will walk up there and find you and just go in your car."

He hung up and told Ben that Helen was up in the upper lot of the church where she thought that it all had occurred, and that, she wanted to ride along with them for a sandwich.

"I think she's where we were snooping around earlier up where the cars were burned. Let's just walk up and ride in her car and she can bring us back."

They topped the second hill and didn't see Helen's car so Jason called her to ask where she was. Helen answered and said that she was parked in the churches entry parking space.

"I don't see you. Wave your hands or something. maybe you're in the wrong lot."

"No I'm not, I see the two of you now. Do you see me? I'm on your right hand side in front of both of you on the other side of the bikes waving right at you."

"Oh, I see you now, your down at the other end of the church," said Jason.

They continue to walk towards Helen while she walked towards them. When she got up nearer to them she said,

"You know I thought it happened down at that end of the church where I just parked. Now I see that the burn marks on the ground are way over here. I guess it's kind'a too bad it didn't happen over there where my car is; you would have been able to see what had happened on that camera up there on the roof," she said while pointing up to it.

"My God Helen, I could kiss you! That's the clue I've been dreaming about and never seen it until you pointed it out."

"Did I do good honey?'

"Hey Benjamin, look up there way over on the right hand side of the upper wall of the church."

"Yea, I see it now. Maybe our wise killer has f-d up, huh? Let's get into the church and hope the cameras were turned on and facing this way when he put the child's body into the car."

"I hope the camera was on and I hope it wasn't too dark to see and it may be hard to identify him at that distance if we'll be able to see him at all, said Jason."

The pastor of the church was more than co-operative. He ran

and re-ran the recorded video on his screen that had the capability of light enhancement, slow motion and a freeze status.

The video recorder time was moved back to that night just before Jason and Ben drove up in their cars. Though it was a good distance away you could clearly see Ben's black un-marked car pull up first and, a not so clear frame of him, getting out of the driver's door to make his way to the trunk. Just as he opened the trunk Jason pulled beside him in his silver BMW and joined him. The camera vaguely picked up some of Jason facial features as he walked towards the trunk of Ben's car. They watched as the two men loaded their weapons, shook each other's hands and walked off into the darkness away from the cars. With-in a few minutes they watched as a car, which had been parked where Helen's car was parked in the shadows of the church. His lights were turned on and he slowly drove up behind Ben's and Jason's vehicles. A very big man got out of the driver's seat of what looked to be a white Range Rover. He looked around cautiously and proceeded to the rear door of his own car. After a few more glances around and back up at the church, he then opened the trunk and lifted out a child that had been taped at the ankles and mouth with his arms taped behind his back.

"Holy shit," said Jason "the kid must have still been alive at that point or why would he have bound and gagged him like that".

He sat the child on the ground and searched around and picked up a good sized block or stone and threw it through the rear door widow of Ben's car. He then quickly reached in and unlocked the rear car door. He then grabbed the child's taped arms and threw him into the rear seat. With the car door still open, he knelt down on his knees as if in prayer. After a moment or so, he seemed to speak to the child as he reached in and handled him roughly while appearing to be speaking upward into the night sky. He then hurriedly walked to his still opened rear door and returned to Ben's rear door. He sprinkled some kind of liquid inside onto the boy's now kicking body. He slammed the door shut and threw the remaining liquid in through the broken out window.

"I keep wanting to run out there and shoot his ass about nine times and recue the boy. I keep forgetting that what we're seeing has already occurred."

"Me too," said Ben.

After striking a match and igniting the apparently flammable liquid he stood back and raised both of his arms into the air while looking up into the heavens. He was talking to the night skies while retracting and lifting his arms again and again. Finally, he motioned his hands towards the burning car in a way that indicated giving something away. He began to speed up his movement while taking one final look around to see if he may have been seen. He seemed to have looked directly up at the camera and smiled.

"Wait, hold that frame!" Ben shouted "Can you blow that shot up as close as you can get it?" In that brief movement the reflection of light shined on his face. "Look, he has blood red eyes and he's smiling right at us, or the camera."

The man then returned to his car and drove off into the night.

The hearts of both of the Alpha males were throbbing with a desire to rip the head off of this monster as pure revenge.

"Benjamin, we've got to get this man, or devil, whatever he is; we've got to get him."

"I know, I feel the same way. It will be a blessing for me to shove my pistol down his throat or up his ass and empty it."

The minister spoke up. "He seemed to be performing some kind of sacrificial ritual to the devil or something."

"I noticed", Ben said. "I'm going to need this video to see if we can enhance it enough to make out more of what he looks like and who he might be. He was a white male dressed in what looked like a doctor's uniform. Other than those two positive observations I couldn't determine much more."

"I noticed that he had on a surgical cap and cloves. The type they wear at a hospital operating room. His car, I think was a white or maybe silver Land Rover," said Jason.

"Yea that's right, it looked silver but it was hard to tell in that bit of light. Well, we can analyze it much better down at the police station. I need something so I can put a name and address on this fucker. Mainly so I can stop gritting my teeth," said Ben.

Chapter Twelve

After leaving the church and having a sandwich with more than fifty people, Helen, Ben and Jason returned and sat in Helen's car talking.

"You know Benjamin, this all seems more unreal than all of the other escapades of our past including those that Esha and Oz played a role in. The reason is it's twisted with some things that are un-godly and more than man-evil.

While we were watching our Locust killer at work I could almost swear to you that there were eyes of something evil watching all of us including him. In my mind he was smiling in approval of what was happening. Even more so, I think he realized that we were too late. I know there is no such thing as devils and demons but yet, our bible teaches us that there are other gods. Two of such gods come to mind that you may or may not have heard of. One was Molech, he received child sacrifices. The other was a god of fertility that supposedly had involvement with Molech; I think her name was Ezar or something like that."

"I don't know," Ben said while still gazing out of the car window with a very angry face. "I'm still puzzled as to, where could the children have come from. Why they're not on any list of missing children? Obviously they are all about the same age. For me this is the world's greatest mystery that we must solve or all of our own anger will be wasted on frustration. I don't quite know why at the moment, but

I think we should follow up on Helen's theory about the possibility of someone stealing children as either as infants or prior to them being born," said Ben.

He couldn't imagine in his wildest dreams how so many children could be missing and go un-reported. The children found dead at the church had still not been identified and probably never would be.

Jason was obsessed with the killings. It's all he could think about in his sleep and while awake. With Helen present and listening he began to think out loud with a bombardment of questions.

"How could it happen with today's muti-media devices at our disposal? Why can't we match any of these children a list of the missing anywhere that's accessible to us? How could they have been gathered from three different nationalities without a clue of how he brought them together? Could it be a cult?" Jason's gut feeling told him that this guy works alone because he felt that it would be a hard secret to keep among any group of people. He felt that someone along the line would eventually speak up and brag. He wondered about a rich man that could afford to buy the un-wanted or a social worker that could trick the system into thinking the children could have been relocated. Or, how about a drug cartel, that could trade children for drugs? Maybe there is an underground link to a man-boy association that is in position to pull this kind of crime off by convincing there members that this is a good way of providing them with good candidates and rejecting all those that are not of Europeans descent. Or, I don't know, maybe it's some of all above. I have to think that whoever it was that committed these murders had to live in the Pittsburgh area. How could he have pulled it off? We've ran photos of those that could be recognizable without any response from anyone in the tri-state area. Jason stopped brainstorming by himself and asked Helen her feelings of any reasonable possibility.

"Well, thank you for asking. I kind'a think for some reason as I told you and Jason earlier, that they may have been kidnapped at a much earlier age and held somewhere until they reach an age suitable for young sexual activity. I've even thought of the possibility that they could have been taken as infants or even prior to birth. I don't know if the last thought could be possible unless it was done by a team of doctors and nurses. I don't know how or why certain races seems to be a factor, but I agree that they were rejected rather than chosen. Maybe that's why their corpse was treated so badly. Maybe they were racially hated or not desirable enough to keep. Whatever the case,

I think they were captive long enough to make them impossible to identify by the police."

"I don't know if any of those thoughts have any factual merits mainly because all those factors would require a number of involved people that I think would have exposed each other somewhere along the line.

I'm thinking that if our killer has struck elsewhere with the same m.o. it could mean several things; one that he has moved on to another place and we may never see him again. Two, that, if it's found to be true that he kills every seven years, this case will go cold and probably nothing similar will occur in this jurisdiction. Three, and most importantly Ben and I can leave no stone unturned to get him right now."

"Why aren't you getting a clue from Oz or Esha? What are they doing while these people snatch these children? Why aren't they acting with revenge for these murdered children as they have in the past? Where are they now Jason," asked Helen.

"I don't know. I haven't knowingly been possessed for at least six months and you always know when and if I leave out at night looking like the hulk with my blackened eyes and my shirt bursting like its three sizes too small. I have no answers just questions just like you. But I'm getting mentally stuck on your theory of the possibility of infants being kidnapped," said Jason.

Later Jason spoke with Ben. "Yes you heard me right. Helen has more on her theory that she is checking out as we speak. I'm a little afraid to think of it and, yes it sounds farfetched, but she has a better possibility than both of us so far. If these babies were taken before birth it would explain a lot things especially if they were taken by the trickery of being convinced of a necessary abortion."

"My God Jason; as harsh as that sounds and as sick as it would be; I agree, it fits and solve a lot of question here at the station. Most all it would be a full proof way to hide the children's existence. It would also explain why Oz or Esha couldn't hear their pleas in same manner as other murdered children. That night at the catch basin, only one child's voice and Esha tried but couldn't confirm the child killer as usual. That may be why he didn't return to make the kill himself. Maybe, just maybe, he could not be summoned clearly because the child was sacrifice for a god. Could it be that someone could steal the un-born and keep them alive for sacrifice at a later date?"

"That's it Ben, that's what has happened I feel this one in my soul.

The age of their sacrifice must be around seven years of age, or like the old adage that eight is too late. It could be that African born and the Asian or Hispanic may be un-acceptable to their god so they may have dumped them after the common torture and sexual abuse.

This is the one possibility that could explain more than a few things. If a doctor, in the privacy of his own office were to tell an expectant mother that her child has for some reason died after being carried six or seven months inside the womb, she would grieve but ultimately yield to the removal of the fetus for her own health. I guess the next question would be what happens to the supposedly deceased fetus in typical cases."

"From my understanding the mother to be is given the choice of letting the doctor have it to dispose of or making funeral arrangements at her own expense; which would probably cost thousands of dollars. If the mother choses to let the hospital do what it does, the doctor could easily take the living infant and keep it alive for a different purpose, like nurturing it for the purpose of sacrifice somewhere other than the hospital. That would give a nut like we have; an opportunity to get possession of babies and no one would suspect a thing. Not only that, he would also be able to choose the race and nationality of the infant base upon that of the mother, that's if for some reason nationality makes a difference in his purpose."

"That certainly would explain why there is no missing child report and it may explain why the children at the church were of different nationalities. It looks like we're on to something," said Jason. "Why don't we check to see what equipment that might be used to sustain the life of a fetus? It's probably the same apparatus that's used as life support for premature babies in the maternity ward at the hospitals. Then, maybe if we're lucky we can track down who may have purchased the equipment."

"That's a dam good start," said Ben. "I can't even begin to imagine how many abortions there have been in the last thirty years here in western Pennsylvania."

"Well I'm hoping that there is a company that may have bought some of the essentials for resale or maybe have kept records of a buyer that can lead us to a suspect. I'm pretty sure an incubator is not manufactured for public use. For now this is our best chance and it's starting to be more of a possibility than you or I could have imagined," said Jason.

"This may be more than a possibility; it could turn quickly into a probability if we find the seller and the buyer. Why don't you see what additional information Helen or the other girl can come up with?" said Ben.

"This is all so crazy. Just to think like me; a lot of people reason that our Creator should have spoken out much louder against pedophilia or clarify laws pertaining to the abuse of children. I'm sure you've heard about folk that talk about sparing the rod and spoiling the child; I personally think that's bullshit. There is always a way to teach without finding the need to physically beat and maim another person.

I'm saying that the Creator was clueless when it comes to the perverseness and cruelty that mankind became able to conjure up in his own despicable mind. How do you think that the Creator of love and compassion could create something inside of some of us that can disregard God's nature of things and implement abominations like anal sexual lust from one man to another or towards infants and children? I don't believe that the same creator could turn that coin and make it ideologically possible.

I believe that, like many other misery causing diseases, pedophilia has contaminated man's mind and has grown and has run rampant without a cure at hand. Mankind has abused God's gift of freedom to be fruitful and to multiply, to the need to satisfy his own desire to become Godlike and rule."

"Well," Ben said "they must have access to some kind of incubator that they manage to keep in secrecy. That's what I'm thinking. For their god, some people would defiantly keep their mouths closed for fear of some super natural retaliation. It all adds up. Now we, meaning you and I, not Oz and Esha, must take the so called locust killer down with all those around him."

"Do you think you and I can be cold blooded enough to make the kill of more than one human if there's a group of them"

"Yes."

Chapter Thirteen

Helen spent the next three days following up on organizations that customarily buy used hospital equipment in the tri-state area. There were three; one of them was located in the area just southwest of Pittsburgh near the West Virginia state line. Another of them was a surgical scrap dealer and the third was listed as a salvage company that repaired and resold to private hospitals and doctors.

Helen called Jason upon finding the possible lead.

"Hey, I found one company located not far from here by the name of Second Best. I called and asked them if they sold reconditioned incubators or any other kind of life sustaining equipment and they responded that they did. They said that has been their specialty for more than forty years of the family business. I attempted to get more information by asking what kind of companies they sold to; he said while attempting a scary sounding voice 'we sell to Dr. Frankenstein type doctors that want to bring back the dead. And sometimes we sell to zombies,' then he laughed out loud and said, 'no seriously, we usually sell to private doctors with specialty services. We guarantee everything that we sell with a one year warranty and he went on and on about the quality of their products.' I asked him the price range of an incubator and he said 'they can run as much as twenty five thousand dollars including all of the attachments."

"Can you call back and try to squeeze out the names of some of his buyers," asked Jason.

"I can try, but I doubt it. He sounded like someone that shines them for resale instead of an actual salesman that may know the product and their uses. I will call back and try."

"You know what, never mind. See if you can get me the address, I think I'm going to take a ride over there and see if I can get a feel for what they actually do."

"Okay good, but I'd like to ride with you. I can stop at that wholesale garment place out on Rte. 79 that's on the way."

"Alright, that sounds good, we'll go first thing tomorrow morning," said Jason.

After an hour and a half drive they arrived at the Second Best. The place was located in a small in town just past Washington Pa... The store front appeared to be more of an antique shop than a place that sold surgical equipment. The attached rear building looked big enough to hold a hundred cars.

Helen and Jason walked up to the cluttered sales counter while looking around at the abundance of oxygen tanks and outdated wheelchairs that were parked everywhere.

'Hello, is there anybody here?"

There was no answer so Jason continued to neb around the store front while Helen read some of the family business literature that was taped all over the walls and counter tops. One of the taped on notes read, 'Shop lifting is a crime'

"Why would anyone buy any of this stuff? Most of it looks like it's been here for more than a hundred years and some things even longer. Look," she said "as she pointed at a laundry basket filled with old stethoscopes. I don't believe doctors even use them anymore."

Helen turned around and found Jason sitting in a wheel chair in front of what appeared to be a vintage glass top incubator with tubes coming out of the top and sides.

"Do you want one of those classics?"

An old ladies voice came from a walk way behind the counter.

"We keep some of the stuff around to astonish customers," she said.

Jason seized the opportunity to attempt getting a few coincidental answers that he was looking for.

"Wow, who buys this sort of thing and for what may I ask."

"We don't have a huge demand for incubators even in the newer models," the lady responded.

"What about other life sustaining equipment for premature babies. What could anyone do with that kind of junk, outside of hospitals," was his questioning probe.

"I don't have a clue," she responded, "but; every three or four years we get stuck with them as a part of a 'buy-all' auction."

"Wow." Jason acted astonished.

"As-a-matter-of-fact," the lady said, "some guy comes in here and buys that kind of junk that can only be used to bring back the dead for almost nothing."

Helen and Jason's attention was suddenly drawn to this particular buyer that she was talking about.

"That sounds like the scary man that I was talking to when I called up here yesterday," said Helen.

"No, that's my forty five year old son you must have talked to. He likes to think that a lot of the stuff we sale to folk is used to create zombies and monsters. He means well but sometimes he scares the shit out of children that might come in with our buyers."

Jason kept probing with statements and hidden questions.

"I want this wheel chair I'm sitting in," he said. While looking over at Helen and giving what he thought might be his frightening look.

"For what," Helen quickly asked.

"For my future honey, so you can wheel me around when I'm older; who knows maybe I'll become a big wheel someday."

"That's not funny Jason. The only place I'm going to wheel your ass is over a cliff for the life insurance money," she said while giving him her own evil eye and a little bit of laughter from her and the sales lady.

"Now that's not funny honey, at all, Jason said while directing his attention back to the store owner.

"I know your son must really have a lot of stories to tell about strange men that come in here and buy weird things, in addition to his wild stories about dead men walking, huh?" Jason asked.

"Oh yea… one gentleman told him that he buys the stuff to help him revive pets and other animals that have been struck by cars. I think that's stranger than the zombie notion but you know how some people are about their pets. Some folk think animals are more important than or just as important as people. It's weird to me. I never know why some people would attempt to revive deer and ducks and all those other animals that we find on our dinner table a few weeks later. We all put thousands of animals on our plates for our meals without giving it a second thought. It's all too much for me to think about," she said while circling her pointing finger in the crazy gesture above her head. "You'd be surprised of the things we can sale to freaky customers. In fact one guy comes through here and buys them for next to nothing and we're glad to get rid of them along with some other stuff that can only be used to bring back the dead. What do you folks want?" she asked.

"Well, for one thing," Jason said "I am going to buy this wheel chair. Tell me this though, the guy that buys the-a… what's it called; Incubators, is he a black guy about five feet eight, looks a little like me and drives a white Jeep?"

"Heavens no, he's a very white gentleman more than six feet tall with short blond hair and really handsome I must say. He has a muscular face. Whew… If I were twenty years younger I'd go save animals with him any day."

"Ma, why are you telling these fine folks those filthy tales," her son said while coming out from the back room.

"That's my son Billy… cause he's cuter than your daddy ever was and just my type," she said while looking at Helen and nodding in an attempt to get an amen.

"Ma just stop it, nobody wants to hear your dream love stories."

"No, it's alright," said Jason. "It's hard to imagine such a good looking guy wanting to buy incubators and expensive equipment while driving a beat up old red jeep."

"Mom doesn't know. He drives a white Land Rover that I wish I had, I know that."

"Wow," Jason responded. "Me too, I've always wanted a seventy five thousand dollar car. I'm with you on that one. He must be a doctor or something, that's for sure," said Jason.

"No," he said, "he dresses like a doctor but he's not a just a doctor; he's a coach at one of universities, across the state line.

"That's my kind of guy; how much for the wheeled throne that I'm sitting in?"

"That one is one hundred and twenty five dollars plus tax. Is there anything else you folks would like?"

"Yea; a job as a soccer coach at Ohio State; like your incubator buyer." Jason said still probing for information.

"No, I think his main job is some kind'a baby doctor over in Pittsburgh and he owns a clinic over in nearby West Virginia. I think he said he also teaches fencing at the nearby college. I don't know who would waste their time try'n to be a sword fighter in these days of A-K- 47's and M-16 assault rifles. Can you imagine try'n to kill a bunch of zombies with a pointed sword?"

"Shut up boy," his mother said. "You know darn well there is no such thing as zombies. Carry his wheel chair out to his car and stop trying to scare the young lady about zombies and monsters."

Chapter Fourteen

On the way back to Pittsburgh with an un-needed wheel chair Jason was anxious to get Helen's approval of his tactic for getting information from the two business owners.

"Well," he asked, "what do you think pretty brown woman, did I do a good job getting some facts?"

"I think you did a very good job. You never cease to amaze me honey. I guess I would have taken the female approach and like... just ask the questions I wanted answered."

"Um-m-m, I didn't think of that" Jason said.

"Don't be a cute ass, smarty" she responded with her feminist little smile.

"Seriously, I'll tell you this. I think we're on to something. I'm going to run it by Ben and see if we can come up with a name for our buddy with the white Land Rover."

"I've got a question... Why didn't you just ask the salesman the man's name," she asked while tapping numbers into her cell phone already in hand.

"Um-m-m, I didn't think of that either, but I don't think he knew it and if he did, he probably wouldn't have given it up, that would have been too easy."

"Hello," Helen said into her phone. "This is the young beautiful black woman that just bought the wheelchair for her tall ugly husband. Is this Billy? ... Hey Billy, I was wondering, would you happen to know the name of the tall blond haired gentleman that your mom was talking about? ... Really, that is silly isn't it? Did he have a first name that you might remember, I'm thinking of dumping my husband just to ride in his Land Rover... Yea Billy that is strange... Okay Billy, thank you so much... I will... I'll make sure he's really alive... I'd hate to be riding around with a dead man... Do you have an address for him," she asked as she winked at Jason.

"Oh don't worry about my husband he will probably be riding around in his old wheel chair while I sport the Rover with my dead friend... Yea... that is funny uh? Okay Billy I'll be talk'n to'ya soon. Maybe I'll take you for a ride someday. Again, thank you so much." Helen said as she turned to face Jason. "Now that's undercover tactics for probing for clues."

"You show off. Okay, so what's his name?"

"My new friend Billy said his name is... you guess."

"Will you stop it and just tell me his name, miss detective trying to show me up"

"He said it was something like Molik, or Molech"

The next morning Jason called Ben to inform him of the lead he and Helen had found.

"Good morning Mr. Benjamin, wait to you hear what Helen and I stumble across up in Little Washington Pa."

"I hope its good news. I need a break in the right direction for a change."

"I think it's more than good. I think we've found our Locust killer."

"Are you shit'n me Jason. The last thing I need right now is a joke."

"No, listen we followed up on a lead about a man that's been buying second hand hospital equipment and lucked up and found a buyer that not only fits the description but drives a white Land Rover or Range Rover, whatever."

"Do you have an address? It's sounds like we should check him out immediately."

"As a matter of fact, thanks to Helen's show off detective work, we do."

"Get out 'a here, no way... where is he located?"

"Helen followed up and found out a man with his name owns an animal rescue and pet hotel at a place just across the Pennsylvania state line called Triadelphia West Virginia."

"Hey I heard of that place; when I was a young boy my dad had relatives there. They used to have an auto race track that drew a big crowd every Saturday night. I know exactly where that is."

"Yea, but the question to you is, are we ready to get'm? We are about to take on a man that thinks he is a god named Molech."

"I don't care what his name is, gods can be killed or taken out of existence forever, I'm sure of it. Am I right Jason, can they be killed?"

"Well we'll have God on our side, how can we lose Benjamin? Plus knowing what we know now he will be much easier to find."

"Let's do it. Give me a time and me and my glock will pick you up. He's my 9mm side kick now and he's always ready for that kind ass hole."

"Its seven a:m right now. Pick me up at my place eight and I'll be ready with my buddies on my side."

"Do we know what he looks like," asked Ben, "or are we just looking this trip?"

"Kind-of; we have a pretty good description. We know for sure he has blond hair with a military type haircut, very broad shoulders and deep inverted eyes. We're guessing his age to be between the ages of forty five to fifty five."

"I'm wondering if I should take the time right now to try and look him up in our records here at the station. It would be hard to believe you managed to get a full name."

"Not exactly, but we're pretty sure that his last name is Molik or Molech like the Old Testament god I was telling you about a couple of days ago."

"You know this is a little scary. It sounds like we have a nut that thinks he's a god. If I spend time having him checked out everyone in the station will know and that would limit our ability to not bring him in alive. I'm thinking we should go up there and see what we will have to go through to bring him back, or at least half way back alive," said Ben. "I'm on my way."

"I'll be in the lot."

Within forty five minutes from the time they met up the two men were headed South on Rte. 79 for Triadelphia.

Other than the typical greetings back in Jason's parking lot, nothing was being said for the first forty minutes of the trip. And then Jason broke the silence.

"How do you feel as police officer that's about to take the law into his own hands; so-to-speak?"

"Well bro I look at it like this. Every time a monster like this one commits a cold blooded crime against a helpless child or any other helpless person, no matter what the age; he makes himself fair game to those of us that feel the need to stand up and protect them by any means available to us. Saying that, I'll tell you exactly how I feel... I feel over anxious. I would like to take the threat away permanently and know that putting a child molester away for couple of years only gives him enough time to figure out how he got caught at it. I believe, and I know I've told you this before, a cruel murdering pedophile has convinced himself that he has every right to have sex with children, and I believe we have every right to kill his ass without a second thought" answered Ben.

"You've said a hell of a lot my friend. What makes me a little frightened is that I'm starting to think like you in so many ways. One of our biggest differences is that you are strongly convinced of your solutions. Your convictions are like that of Oz and Esha; you know what needs to be done and have made up your mind without doubt. Whereas I seem to always be looking for reasons to consider causes and solutions without focusing on how we should simply put them out of their misery by throwing the bad guy directly under the bus. Do you think I'm a pussy or a lion like the rest of the human sides of the ten?"

"Well my brother, I look at it this way; there are sometimes many ways to solve the same problem. We can disagree about many things. I'm right your wrong, or vice-versa. The bottom line is what is truly right. I want to do what is right and many times I believe my conclusions are absolute and then you and I talk, I hear another view and the absolute becomes questionable without a doubt."

"In that case let me run my weakening thought by you, man to man. I've been convinced that the acts of Oz and Esha and the rest of the Ten to protect the defenseless, leads to being rare and excepted by the sons of God in every way. Yet...I know that's not being taught in today's society. I've read that when it comes to sexually molesting babies, God Himself was clueless of the possibility that man could be so cruel. I guess that's why there doesn't seem to be a biblical approach as to how we should deal with it. I believe that it's one of those acts that asking for forgiveness is not an option. I'm just like you, Oz and the others; I feel that if they do it they should die. I think it should be made clear to all; kind-of like jumping off of a cliff, what's in-store for the jumper is obvious, he dies when he hits the ground and so should the natural consequences of a child rapist. If they do it they should die at it. Then you have those who reason that like the serpent, supposedly said to Eve, 'you shale not surely die'. This kind of mind set may have given some people the idea that no matter what evil you commit you will not truly be killed for doing so. And now we are here saying very loudly, yes you will! My wimpy side just needs to know that it will always be the guilty one and not just the accused."

"Yea Bro, that might be the way it should work but that, 'ask and you will be forgiven' approach does not sit well with the dead children or those that loved them. I've been a police officer for twenty sump'n years. I've seen it all. Some men are so cruel and despicable that they know they should die for the crime they committed. Yet, if no one stops them they will do it again and again without giving it a second thought. They all think they will be able to step on some kind of base and holler 'I'm safe' like it's a baseball game, and then step off and do it again. Not on my watch. I want them to know that step'n on the base will not keep you safe from the likes of you and me, let alone Oz, Esha or the rest of the ten. I say let's kill this fool before he kills again. I'm willing to commit this crime, if you want to call it that, without getting caught... I hope."

"Okay... I'm with you, but if you get me caught Helen's going to kill your ass that's for sure. You know... all jokes aside, there's a ninety nine point nine percent chance that this is our man. How do you want to take him down?"

"When I think of all those bodies of those helpless children I just want to walk up to him shooting as many bullets in him as my glock nine will allow. After that you can arrest him or do whatever you think is legal."

"Don't be funny. You know you'd have to read him his rights before you start shooting and by then me and Bet-Lou will have given him to his god Molech or whatever his name is. So you had better read quickly."

"Oh yea, that's right, I've got to read him his rights while you violate his rights, that's not gon'na happen. I would have to arrest you my friend. Just wait and see, it will be more like this; 'Mr. Molech I'm given you the right to remain silent forever', and then you hear a loud boom, boom, boom and its over; no more bad guy," said Ben in a jesting way.

"There you go again, a police officer take'n the law into his own hands. I may have to make a citizen's arrest on you sir."

Jason was thinking very hard for a few moments about what Ben and he had just been joking about. He realized that the laws are not a joke. They are there for a reason. He was taught that laws protect the innocent just as Ben and he were somewhat attempting to do on behalf of the children that were murdered.

"Wait, I have one more question for you Benjamin. About a week ago right before this venture started, Helen asked me, 'why do I think so many men Rape and abuse babies."

"Yea, well I have the same question for you right now, why do so many of these assholes rape babies and often times their own children. Why do they… huh? You answer that please, for Helen and I, and I'll give you a nice shinny nickel."

"Of course you know I don't have a good or satisfying answer to that question. But… you know me I'm like detective Clayton down in D.C., I'd like to try. Number one; I believe that some men are cursed with the burden of wanting to be powerful and feared by others of any age or gender. Of course the easiest victims are children. Number two; there are men that are weak in the deepest part of their soul. They will quickly and gladly give-in to the temptation of their own forbidden and perverted sexual desires at the first opportunity, especially if they believed they can get away with it. They do it without thought of the possible consequences or the harm to the children. They, just simply put, are incapable of resisting their own selfish urges. Thirdly, I believe that there are those that thirst to inflict the worst of pain upon people of good spirit just because they stand to condemn the devious acts that they've come to live by, and again, children are the easiest targets. These men commit abominations against everything spiritual including powers that hate and have no moral connection to anything that exist. They even challenge the Most High and His ability to do anything about it; kind of an 'in your face act in an attempt to aggravate everyone's God regardless of their religious beliefs. I'm trying to convince myself that we are justified to hunt them down and take their threat away from all of our children. I want to declare war against every one of them both near and far. Their natural instincts for evil acts cannot be dealt with by reasoning or compassionate pleas from their victims. Most or all diseases worsen if not attended to. They grow, infect and kill when there is no defensive mechanism in place or, in this case, no man to stand in their way."

"Wait now, I have a serious question for you," said Ben.

"Come on with it."

"I've never known you to be a religious man especially knowing that you were in the U.S. Marines as a sniper. There, you had obligations to fight and kill for your comrades and country. In fact, when we were growing up as kids; I never knew you or your family to even go to church. I've noticed that since the ten angels have come together as a child predator task force, and have been, what you might say, using our human bodies without our permission and sometimes without our knowledge; you've based most of your thoughts and decision on biblical history. What's gone on with that? I mean, I know our mysterious experiences with the likes of the angelic Esha and Oz has added a new dimension of possibility that's far beyond our understanding, but how do we know they are God sent. They may be of an evil spirit within us that exist in some of mankind. I find it interesting that you and Oz seem to have been chosen to lead this roller coaster ride of fighting an ultimate evil. You are practical and you always try to show compassion. Oz, at least what we think we know of him, is cunning and seemingly on a mission to weed out known child predators based upon his gift of having the ability to communicate with dead kids. That's a gift that most of us humans don't have. Is it you and I my lifelong friend, are these missions of revenge being planted in our spirits by murdered children, or is it maybe Jehovah's wish for some reason to use us as tools with and without our angelic counterpart?"

Jason pondered the series of question by Ben as if it were the first time he had given them any thought of his own.

"Man Benjamin," he said while taking a deep breath. "I have asked that question to myself. I know I've not been a very religious man to say the least. In fact I've been driven inside to answer those same questions that are very vague and unclear too me in a logical sense. My common senses have caused me to question biblical beliefs ever since I've learned to read for myself. Before Oz came along the only voices I heard were my own, usually while talking in my sleep on the verge of waking-up. When I was a small child I often heard voices of other children but I could not make any sense of them and they often gave me nightmares that I can still remember very well. As a teenager I began to recognize that I should be brave and heroic enough to protect our neighborhood from boys from different parts of the city. I guess I was learning to be territorial. Your right, I had no idea that God or any other supreme being had any influence on our lives. Old people used to say to me, 'boy your bad little ass needs to go'ta church and pray.' My mother used to constantly tell me, 'God's watching you; you'd better behave or-else.' I often wondered what or-else meant but I had no fear of it whatever it might be. In-fact I wanted to fight who or whatever 'or-else' was just to prove I could take him down. Right now and over the past three or four years I have found a prayer that fits what I believe in. That is, my desire to right every wrong committed against women and children or anyone that's being bullied by uncaring people to the point that they've lost their rights to pursue happiness. I guess I want to be a real hero or something, so I pray for it even though I've had no personal relationship with God outside of Him saving my life a thousand times or making my life worth living every day, I want give something back."

Jason paused as if reluctant to expose his personal disagreements with God.

"In my mind, and sometimes out loud when no one is around to hear, I say to God or your Jehovah, why are you letting these bad things happen while you sit on your throne. My questions especially occur during those times when I read or heard of something that only a devil or someone evil could have done. I say: don't you laugh Ben, I say, use me God to fight for what is right. Let me kill the devil and his servants that are filled with hatred and jealousy. I wanted to be God's soldier because I've never been smart enough to be afraid of those that harm others. I actually thought that I was the biggest and strongest of all of God's soldiers and I would never give up until they were harmless to all or put back into hell where they belong. Isn't it silly that I would wish to fight for a God that I never learned to worship? Somehow I knew that I could rest assure that if I'm fighting on your God's team I would always win. I thought He would take me into heaven in spite of my resistance to becoming a so called holy roller or obsessed prayer rituals."

"Well my friend," said Ben, "maybe your prayers have been answered. We are most definitely going after the worst kind of man that exists. I've got a feeling that this guy won't just come along peacefully. I think he is also cunning and well trained by his own god to ward off men like you and I Bro. The reasoning for him is that he hates the same God that we love even though we all love Him in deferent ways. It seems to me a rapist has turned his back on the idea of living in harmony and respecting the rights and feelings of others.

He has adjusted to his own selfishness no matter what the damage he needs to do to acquire it"

"I think so too. So I guess, like in biblical days, it's a matter of who's God is the strongest or who's servant is more dedicated. Do you pray Benjamin?"

"Of course I do. You know I was raised as a Jehovah's Witness. Prayer means everything"

"This time can you say a little one for me too while you're at it. I still think He's not listening to me. When I whisper into His ear for some kind of sign I never seem to get one that I'm sure is coming from Him."

"That's because you don't follow the rules like us Jehovah Witnesses," Ben said as a joke and made himself laugh at his own comment.

"Answer this my friend; If you had the choice of going to hell or heaven as you know them or staying right here on earth just as it is forever, which one would you choose?"

"Well, I'm a coward like everybody else that I know. I would choose to stay right here amidst all of happiness and misery that we as people can conjure up. But I would think most people would choose heaven. I don't think hell would get any votes."

"Okay now… what if you were given the choice of the paths that it takes to get to those destinations. Things like, daily prayer, worship every Sunday, being quick to forgive others, avoiding the biblical sins, you get my drift. Would you choose the path that you must take to get you to your place of choice or the known path to death forever, that place we know as hell that we've heard so much about? Come on Bro… tell the truth."

Jason chuckled and looked at Ben with a tilted head as if this was going to be a trick question.

"In that case I change my choice, even though I'd probably be hell bound like everybody else that's a child of blindness. You know what… on second thought I don't want to choose my path or my destination. I just want to put trust in God that He will understand enough to place me somewhere in His school of learning until I get it right."

"That's not an answer. You just pulled off one of your same ole answers that place the blame on someone else."

"Yea, well that's my answer to you. God and I have an understanding that you will never understand. I would still choose to stay right here on earth but I would probably in up in hell with you."

"Yea, well I know where your ass is going, and I won't be there, and you better be ready for a long hot stay," Ben said in a joking way.

"You know... as long as you're right by my side I think we'll do what's best where ever we are."

"Bull shit... I said, I'm not go'n with you. It's enough to have to put up with your trouble making here. Anyway, I'm blessed as a peace maker I deserve a break"

"What you should know is that bad guys are cursed because you're a peace keeper that takes no bull. Hey... I'm proud of you."

Chapter Fifteen

"We're almost there according to the gps," said Jason.

They got off of the main highway and made several turns as the gps directed and ended up in a small town just outside of Triadelphia dividing West Virginia and Pennsylvania. A rural one street town surrounded by homes located about a mile apart.

"What's the plan Benjamin?"

"I plan on driving up to his house and asking him why he did it and how he thought he would get away with it. And then, if no one is in harm's way; I'm just going to shoot him in the face."

"Dam Benjamin! I guess that is a plan... but don't you think we should somehow first introduce ourselves and make sure he's our man."

"Yea, after we shoot'em a few times, we can ask him kindly, if he did it. Bro, listen to me; you and I both know that this is the killer. I can feel it in my bones. Everything fits, we just don't know why or how he's been doing and getting away with it or how long he's been doing it. If we have the right man the Locust killings will stop, if not, they'll continue, it's as simple as that when it comes to proof."

"Benjamin, I know you're kidding but just in case I want you to know that I don't agree. My instinct tells me that he is the culprit, but the seven years apart killings won't stop until we break the habits of the cult, the whole cult. I think we have to expose the whole system that's behind the child sacrificing. Maybe with help from above and today's media we can spearhead the down fall, or at least make others aware of a false belief that child rapists have both knowingly and unknowingly lined up to be a part of."

"So, you think that you and I alone can track down the players of a child, let me get this right, a child pedophile slash, religious cult, slash, biblical curse all over the world; just you and me as Ben and Jason?"

"Well... maybe you with Esha, and me with the help of Oz and the other eight angels if needed. I'm saying maybe, just maybe, we can make them know that their secret society has been exposed and, like you said, we start taking some of them out of the loop with bullets up their, you know what."

"Oh now you don't want to cuss. Asses that's what!" said Ben, "That's the one part that I agree with whole heartedly"

"Okay, I guess that's as good a spot as any to fire a couple rounds.

According to the gps we'll be coming up on the address we're looking for within five miles. I don't see anything but corn fields and trees. The road is getting narrower," Jason said.

"Up ahead four or five miles it looks like we're coming to a dead end like the sign said when we entered onto this red dog covered road about a mile or so back. And it looks like the mountain up in front of us just pushed right up out of the farm land telling us we won't be going much farther unless we're mountain climbers."

"There's a sign posted that says 'private drive way, do not enter.'"

"That came with no warning until now," Ben remarked.

"What are you doing?

Ben had pulled over to the side of the road and grabbed a pair of binoculars from the glove compartment.

"When we first came onto this country road, I don't know if you noticed but there was a huge old white church on our left as we made the right hand turn. Then came what too looked like a community grave site followed by a horse stables and then some kind of pet vacation place according to the sign at the drive way entrance. And then we passed about two miles of corn fields all along the way on our right hand side. Now we're coming to a dead end with nowhere else to go but through that white gate that's a good ways up ahead in front of us that must lead to our destination."

"Now what are you doing"

"The whole distance to here we had nothing but corn fields and abandoned railroad tracks on our right. I saw tracks going up into the corn about a half mile back. I'm gon'na back up and try and hide our vehicle up in the corn stocks and we'll have to walk to the house from there on foot."

"Okay, so now the detective is coming out in you and I like it as well as being impressed like hell. So... we're going to walk to the gate rather than drive through like gang buster on TV... That doesn't sound like the Ben I've come to know but I really like the idea none the less. I too think we have a much better chance to surprise him walking in unseen. So, let's do it my friend."

They drove the car diagonally up into the six or seven feet high corn stocks getting it out of sight of any passing car that might be coming one way or the other. Once out of the car they both checked and pack their weapons of choice including Ben's marksman's rifle and proceeded towards the big white gate to nowhere.

Chapter Sixteen

After walking about one half mile keeping out of sight, they heard oncoming cars and backed up a little deeper into the corn. Two cars came roaring by kicking up dust and small stone as if they were running from the law. Right behind the first two cars came the white Range Rover. Ben spotted the driver and a female in the passenger seat of the Rover. Jason verified that the driver did fit the description of their suspect without noticing the female at all.

After it had appeared that all the cars had passed, they emerged and walked the remaining short distance across the fully mowed grass along the road way and up to the gate. The gate was locked by a remote control device. The house was in full view about two hundred yards from where they stood. It was an average size home, seemingly built right up against the foot of the looming mountain of sand stone cover by pine trees which were protruding straight up behind it all the way up to the blue sky above. There were no remaining cars in the front or side gravel covered parking lots. There was, however, a huge newly converted ambulance truck parked up against the far left side of the house. Jason picked up a stone and jammed it into the mechanism of the gate so that it would not open while they were down inside of the house investigating.

With guns drawn they both cautiously walked down and approached the right side of the house opposite to the ambulance truck. Ben walked around to the front door while Jason took to the windows on the side. There did not appear to be anyone left inside. Ben opened the rot iron storm door and knocked as hard as he could. There was no response. He knocked again while shouting, "hello; is there anyone home?" There was no answer from within. Jason walked pass Ben to the left side of the house. The big converted ambulance was bumped totally against the house so tightly that neither the side of the ambulance nor the entire side of the white aluminum clad house could be seen. He walked pass the entire length of the truck in an attempt to view the rear of the home, only to find that the rear of the truck and the home seemed to be buried into the base of the mountain side up past the roof. Jason returned to the front in time to hear Ben say that he didn't believe anyone was home. They both continued back to the right side while attempting to open the windows.

"Well, no one is here what do you want to do Benjamin," he asked just as Ben took his elbow and broke the glass window pane.

"Okay, I guess we're going to break the window and go in."

Before Jason could say another word Ben had already climbed through the now opened window and had unlocked the front door for him to enter.

"We need to look around and find something that ties this place to the missing children, so let's get busy. You walk back up to the gate and make sure it's jammed so we don't get surprised and on the way listen out for any cars that might be coming back and I'll start looking around for evidence."

By the time Jason went back up to the gate and returned; Ben was sitting in the kitchen drinking a soda from a bottle.

"What took you so dam long it was kind of scary in this place alone?"

"Oh yea, why, what did you find Mr. brave police man from the city?"

"I found a lot of things and nothing. Most of which don't make any sense. For example, two of the bedrooms remind me of a furniture store show room. They are in perfect order, there clean and have everything picture perfect from the made up beds to the pictures on the walls. There are boxes of tissue on the night stand unopened. Brand new shoes lined up under the bed nicely placed side by side. A comb and brush on the dresser that's obviously never been used. There's a newspaper, The Pittsburgh Press, dated seven years ago, that's looks as if it's never been read. No clothes in the closets, a robe hanging on a hook on the back of the bathroom door. Inside of the bathroom there's a completely burnt out cigarette that obviously burned through without being puffed. Everything, including bars of soap and un-used tubes of toothpaste are just sitting there waiting for a mannequin to fit right in. The refrigerator is filled with soda pop, beer and bottled water. There is no food in the cabinets, no dishes, no silver ware, nothing that indicates daily human use."

"Well, what's in the back rooms," Jason asked.

"I didn't get that far; I got thirsty and decided to wait for you."

Jason headed for the back bedroom doors with Bet-lue up against his chest like it was a television scene. The door was locked from the inside so he tried the other door and it too was locked.

Chapter Seventeen

"These doors in the back aren't like the front bedroom doors; they're both made of heavy metal and have double dead bolt locks."

"Stand back a little," Ben said, "I'm just going to kick the dam things in." He put his back towards the door and back kicked against it as hard as he could with the heel of his right foot. It didn't budge. He kicked it again and again. There was not even a crack in the casing. He then tried the same thing on the adjacent door with the same results. Jason was watching and listening while walking back and forth from front to back keeping an eye on the driveway out front and Ben's activities with the two doors at the rear of the house.

"What are we going to tell these folk if they come and find us in their living room," asked Jason.

"I don't have a clue, but I'm sure you'll think of something Bro. Hopefully we'll find something incriminating enough to just stay and make their day by disrupting all the evil shit they've been doing or... maybe they won't come home before we leave and go on our merry way."

After almost fifteen minutes of kicking, pushing and grunting on the back bedroom doors, Ben gave up and said,

"Fuck this, let's go around the side and break in through one of the rear side windows. You keep lookout again while I try the rear section window."

"You know I keep thinking you're going to get us caught and thrown in jail if I keep listening to your ideas. So... hurry up and get in before someone does come through the gate before we're ready... Please."

Jason walked about fifty feet up towards the gate before hearing the glass break. He turned and waited a few minutes expecting to see Ben grinning at the front door waving him in. Instead, Ben came into view from the same side he had walked away from, motioning for him to come back.

"Look at what's inside of the rear window. This shit is truly amazing."

Jason walked up to the big gaping hole that Ben knocked in the lower window and looked inside.

"What do you think of this?"

"Holly shit, what the hell is that," Jason asked while pointing at the dirt filed room.

"I don't know. It looks like the mountain above has slid down and filled the house with stone and dirt."

"But that can't be it would have crushed the house roof and all, not just seeped into the back windows and slowly fill up the room. I've never seen anything like this in my life. No wonder you couldn't push the bedroom doors open. The doors are packed with soil against them. The roof itself is embedded into the mountain side. All I can say is wow."

They walked to the other side of the house. They hadn't noticed before but not only the rear of the house, but also almost ten feet of the ambulance truck was embedded into the mountain base. Yet, nothing was crushed it was all just simply buried. They both backed away from the house far enough to see the bigger picture. The house and truck together was banked into the foot of the mountain but appeared to be sitting just in front of it at a distance of about fifty feet.

"I'm puzzled. This all seems like a stage setting for a play. That's why the inside has been unlived in and so mysterious."

"Jason there's a car coming towards the gates. Hurry let's get out of sight."

The white Rover pulled up to the gate and momentarily sat waiting for it to open electronically. Jason had done a good job jamming the device so that it wouldn't open. After a few moments they both watched while hidden behind some nearby brush on the truck side of the house as their man grabbed a large duffle bag, walked around the gate and headed down towards the house.

"That's our man," said Ben. Let's just stay back until he goes inside then we'll rush in and over take him using the element of surprise and take care of this creep."

"I got'cha boss"

"Sh-h-h let him go all the way in. Get ready Jason."

When the suspect reached about twenty feet from the door he turn towards them and slightly left and headed for the truck on the opposite side of where they were waiting to rush in behind him with their ambush. After a few seconds they heard what sounded like a small truck start up and drive off. They eased around the front porch to the other side to see where he might be. Only to find no one there and nothing disturbed.

"Where in the hell did he go," Ben asked.

Jason did not answer. They looked at each other at the same time and then headed back up towards the gate where he had parked. "We must have been spotted," said Ben, as they both began to run towards the Rover as fast as they could. "Let's go! Go, go, go, we can't let him get away!"

When they got to the car it was empty and untouched with the keys hanging in the ignition. There were three infant car seats in the rear seat. Ben walked to the rear of the car and popped the trunk while Jason kept watch on the house through the binoculars.

"Well... what's taking you so long? What's back there? Why is it taking you so long to say something?"

"Hey Jason look at this. Come back here and see for yourself what you make of this."

"Oh no, I hope not more puzzling surprises, this is getting ridiculous, what is it now?" Jason asked, while not taking his eyes off of the house.

"I don't quite know. There's about three boxes of depends, baby formula, a couple of oxygen tanks and a lot bandage tape. And there are a lot of those plastic containers they use to feed you intravenously when you're lying in a hospital bed."

"That may explain the stationary ambulance down against the house. Maybe this guy is some kind of whacko doctor."

Jason opened the passenger door and looked inside the glove compartment.

"Here's a box of 45 cal. bullets, no gun. Some hypodermic

needles, uh huh, this is interesting there's an owner's card in the name of Dr. Isaac Molech. Obviously this guy is either a real doctor or a nut that's trying to live up to his god's name."

The two men walked back towards the house along the higher grass where they could not be seen as easily. While walking they kept their eyes on the side of the house where they had last seen their vanishing suspect.

As they came up upon the ambulance side of the house they drew their weapons and slowly proceeded. The left side of the passenger door that had been padlocked closed still was. The driver's side door was pressed flush up against the house with no space for access. The windshield revealed an inner door that led back to the box body of the truck and was in sight and undisturbed. It appeared that the only place he could have gone was straight up the mountain side and there was no visual evidence that anyone had climbed the steep grade at that point. He just simply vanished and left both men puzzled. "I'm starting to feel like we're being watched," said Ben.

"That's strange because so am I, and it doesn't feel good at all. I don't see any cameras or anything resembling a place to hide one on this side of the house. Let's back up and wait for a while to see what may happen next. It's not even noon yet so we have a lot of daylight left."

"Maybe he spotted us and walked along the tree line to get away," said Ben. "Remember he knows what you and I look like."

"Yea, well where in the fuck did he go that quickly that we did not see him and what about the sound of the small motor that we both heard before we came around to this side."

"I don't know," answered Ben.

"Did you feel that?"

"Feel what?"

"There it goes again. The ground is vibrating beneath my feet. Quick, duck down!"

They both fell to the ground out of sight as the entire front of the ambulance swung upwards and opened up. The suspect stepped out of the truck and reached up and closed it behind him. He then, after looking around as if he heard something, and then he briskly started walking back towards the Rover. Jason attempted to get up and Ben pulled him back down into the brush.

"Wait," he said, "Let him go for now. We need to see what and who else might be in that ambulance truck."

"Why don't we just get him now and drag him back inside and do away with him. He may get away if we don't act right now."

"He doesn't know we're here. He didn't go into the house at all and we left the car just as he left it. Go with me on this one Jason. He'll be coming back and we'll be ready and waiting inside to take him down."

"I hope your right this time Benjamin. If he gets away from us now he may be very hard to find again."

Chapter Eighteen

They both watched as their suspect pulled off in his car. Ben and Jason immediately started searching for an access button to the ambulance door.

"Now how in the hell did he get in and out of here. There is no visible hinge or latch other than the one that's locked with a pad lock that's in plain sight and it's about the biggest pad lock I've ever seen," said Jason.

They both felt and pulled on pieces of metal that was attached to the truck and stuck out even just a little.

"This doesn't make sense, we both saw him come out of there at the front end. There's got to be some kind of button or latch. You know Benjamin, maybe it's one way in and another way out."

With that statement still on his lips he reached under where the common hood latch would be and pulled as hard as he could, bingo, it came up and open just enough for them to bend down and go under it to get in. Jason went in first with Ben right on his tail. When they stepped up into the area where the steering wheel should have been, the hood and grill slammed back into the shut position with both of them standing inside in total darkness.

"Now look what you've gotten us into Mr. Benjamin," Jason said while opening his cell phone to give out a little light. Ben did the same with his flip phone.

They quickly realized that they were standing just behind the false windshield of the truck and in front of a locked metal door that lead to the trucks body.

"Stand back," Ben said, "I'm going to see if I can force the door open to see what's on the other side. I hope it's not more mountain dirt."

Unlike the bed room doors inside of the house, the door easily opened when Ben pushed with his shoulder. They were now standing in an inner chamber not much bigger than the first. Low and behold, at about five foot back was the same dirt at a slant from floor to the ceiling of the truck. On the walls were candles and Ivory objects.

"Fuck," said Ben "this nut came in here to worship. He is truly a sick man."

"It looks like some kind of idle worship for a psychopath, but again this also doesn't make any sense. This gives me the creeps even worse than before and it stinks in here. It smells like cow shit."

"Let's get out of here before he locks us in from the outside," said Ben.

"Now how do we get out, seems to be the next good question. The door release has to be over here somewhere. Remember he came out with the whole front end rising up. Put your phone light over here near the real door handle... I don't see anything," said Jason. "Wait I do see something that looks like a small hydraulic jack handle and it has a crank on it. I'm going to give it a turn to see if... ah-uh, there it's opening up the whole front like it did when he came out. I think we've found our way."

The door lifted up like and airplane hatch out and up. The daylight burst through the opening with-in seconds. They both stepped out into the fresh air and leaned against the side of the truck with the door still up and wide open.

"Now that was weird," stated Jason as he looked back inside of what they were thinking was a worship chamber.

"You know he was in there for more than an hour. This makes no sense. A house is filled with dirt and stone. A truck, filled with the same, all for a cooped up place to pray. And, what about the ground vibration we both felt and heard before he came out. What was that all about? And, last but not least, I'm noticing that not one of the many candles around the ivory alter have ever been lit. I wish that was all, but it's not, I'm thinking there must be another door in there somewhere that leads inside of that mountain. There was nothing visible in there that could have shaken the ground like we both felt."

"You know you might be right. Look at the cow shit on the floor, its woven into some kind of netting." Ben got back up into the chamber and used his foot to push the cow shit back against the other wall.

"Look-a-here, look-a-here. There's a stainless steel floor with a lift handle right in the middle of it."

Ben lifted the handle of the door up and pushed it back against the driver's side door and the lights below automatically came on.

The lights exposed a one person doom buggy like shuttle with the key in the ignition.

"Well this explains the ground vibrations," Jason said as he stepped down into the buggy.

"Now let's see where it takes us," he said as Ben looked on.

Jason turned on the key and slightly pushes the throttle.

"It's propelled by a big electric motor. You stay here this time and let me go in to investigate. Hit me on your cell phone if someone comes. I'll communicate with you as I go along to where ever this thing takes me."

"Hey Bro… you know to be safe, no hero shit in there. If there is any kind of problem you come back out and we'll go back in together. I'll give you ten minutes to look around if you're not out I'm coming in."

"That's a deal, in fact make it five minutes; this tunnel can't be that deep into the mountainside. By the way, how are you gon'na come in without my new ride?"

"I'll crawl if I have to. You just go ahead, be safe and get back quickly," Ben seriously said.

Chapter Nineteen

Jason pulled off backwards into the base of the mountain while Ben stood ready and waiting in the secret panel of the ambulance truck.

It took less than two minutes of drive time before Jason came to a stop. The tunnel was about eight feet wide a little over six feet high. He guessed that he had traveled about one hundred fifty feet or so into the mountainside. The junction he had come to was braced up by heavy railroad ties. It appeared to be an old coal mine that had split up into three directions at that point. The junction itself looked to be about twenty feet by twenty feet. It was lit by a crossing string of overhead hanging bulbs. The floor was made up of tightly pack red dog and small pieces of coal.

One of the first things he noticed was a bolt locked heavy timbered door with bright lights shining through the gaps at the bottom and top. He could hear what sounded like some kind of pump motor and bubbling water in the rhythm of a beating heart. An adjacent door looked unlatched but fully closed from where he stood. It was without lights on inside. He slowly walked over and put his ear against the seam of the door and listened. He could clearly hear someone breathing heavily inside. It sounded like a very heavy man's voice with an asthmatic rasped. There was no other sound coming from within. Jason paused and was un-decided whether he should go in alone or go back and get Ben. With his pistol now in hand he pulled on the latch and slowly pulled the door open. It was completely dark inside. He spotted some slight reflections from the lights that were on behind him that indicated that there were light bulbs inside of the room's ceiling. He reached in and felt along the wall where he thought a light switch may be. After feeling around in a circular motion he located a toggle switch and clicked it upward into the on position while continuously focusing into the room's darkest part.

A single dim light hanging overhead revealed a spine tingling sight. It was that of a huge mummified man clad in a bronze like metal from the bottom of his rib cage up to his neck. He was sitting with his legs wide open and the heels of his feet resting on what appeared to be a sacrifice pit. His belly was much larger than the rest of his body and very much out of proportion. He appeared to have a small penis-looking single horn protruding from the center of his forehead with another, which was a little bigger, pointing downward in the place of his chin. He had the breast of pregnant woman that lie down on top of his protruding belly with nipples that pointed away from each other. There was a third horn made of flesh in an upward erect position just below where a naval should be. And… tucked down just under where there should have been testicles, there was clearly a female vagina with no rectum below to be seen. Down under the obvious vagina on the sandstone seat was a pool of a black slimy liquid substance. His bronze covered arms were stretched out in front of his belly as if ready to cradle or draw into his lap whatever may be placed within. Just in front of his sitting position there was the pit. The bottom of the pit was filled with slightly glowing ashes. Above the pit high against the wall was a camera facing the mummified man. Jason found himself tingling with uneasiness as he quickly began backing out of the room while nervously attempting to call Ben on his cell phone. The phone lit up but there was no signal. The mummy's eye's appeared to be following every move that Jason made and suddenly without notice it seemingly turned and grunted out a low pitch noise.

Jason rushed back over to the doom buggy not wanting to look back for fear that someone or thing was about to reach out and grab him from behind. He pulled Bet-Lou back out of his shoulder holster as he jumped up onto the buggy for his hasty retreat. He attempted to get it moving but he was too busy looking back at door and aiming his gun at anything that may have come out behind him. Suddenly a huge shadow moved in front him off to his left. Before realizing that it was just his own shadow, he fired two shots into it only to hear two more shots explode from another weapon into the same shadow.

"What the fuck are we shooting at," yelled Ben, who had entered into the open junction just in front of the buggy while Jason was franticly trying to get it moving.

"I guess we were obviously both shooting at the same shadow. Dam you Ben! I almost shot you."

"Yea I know, and I almost shot-you back... What's gone on? What did you find that's making you look like a scared white man; and get that gun out of my face."

Everything came to a stop. Jason took a deep breath while shaking his head in disbelief.

"I don't know. I seen some weird shit over in that room and panicked trying to get the hell out of there in one piece. I'm okay now but I'll tell you this, this place is freaky like nothing I've ever seen before. That room is a room for making burnt sacrifices and it just blew my mind."

"Okay, settle down and let's go in and take a look together. And... if he's in there we'll do whatever it takes to end this crap right now"

The two of them cautiously walked back into the room with guns in hand.

"My, my, my," said Ben, "I see what you mean. I've never seen a man that big in my life. In addition to all that weird shit glued to him that's making him a man and a woman at the same time he is without an asshole. I guess he could be the missing link between man and woman. He seems to be a dried up corpse with his eye sewed open so he can see us. He's like a huge un-wrapped mummy but he's so fat he looks like he may burst at any minute."

"Look in the pit below his feet," said Jason, "It's half filled with ashes and burned baby body parts."

"Well, I've just noticed something besides all of the scary shit that's obvious."

"What," asked Jason?

"Well it's something simple; all of the wax candles placed around him on the walls. None of the wax is hard yet. These candles were just recently put out. And the baby parts inside of the pit indicate that there were, or still are, additional children being sacrificed. He was in here doing his thing. What we're looking at is part of their worship ritual."

"I know. I think it's supposed to be, or is a replica of Molech. Who was the god I was telling you of that was first read about in the Holly Bible back in the days before Moses. He's the one that demanded child sacrifices for forgiving and the sparing the lives of adults that disobeyed God's commandments pertaining to deviated sexual habits among men. He's also the one that is said to have fooled those that might have contested the sacrifices of live children by having very loud banging drums played during the ceremony to prevent good people from hearing the cries of the children. I guess it could have been considered the loud soul stirring music of the pass. Last but not least, it is written that it was this big fat pig looking god along with a goddess with a name something like Ashtoreth that birthed homosexuality by convincing men that they would be forgiven if they permitted another man to performed anal sex on them. That would be a sacrifice of his male on male virginity. This was believed to be a ritual in honor of a man's childless fertility."

POW, pow, pow. Three gun shots rang out as Ben shot into the head and stomach of the so-called god. Jason looked first at Ben and then up at the mummified body. Pow, pow, pow, pow, went four of Jason's own shots into the body of that beast.

"That truly gave me an enormous sense of satisfaction. Look at that... I'll be dam! He's bleeding from what's left of his left eye socket and above his fat ass belly. How could it actually bleed," questioned Jason.

Jason grabbed his other weapon named George and emptied it into the mummified corpse, as did Ben. When the gun powder smoke lifted there was a distinct view of the riddled corpse that was now slumped over and partially blown apart. Black blood was draining down onto his lower horn and vagina and continuing through his opened legs down into the fiery pit below.

"Did you hear that? I could have sworn I heard him moan or maybe yawn as if we woke the bastard up from a sound sleep."

"I wish I could say I didn't hear anything but I did. I think that's the sound of the blood draining from whatever his ass is. Let's finish looking around. If our friend in the Rover shows up I'm gon'na put him in here with his god only in worse condition. No questions asked."

Chapter Twenty

They closed the door on Molech and approached the door with the bright lights coming from underneath.

"This door looks very strong and it pulls out to open. This is not going to be easy," said Ben. "It's like a jail house door, do you have any ideas?"

"What would happen if we placed a pistol up to the key hole and pulled the trigger?"

"It would probably blow-up in your face. This isn't television you know."

"Well do you have a better idea?"

"Actually… no, I don't; so just do it and shut up."

"Never mind that, I'm going to shoot holes in the wall that the latch goes into on the other side maybe…"

While Jason was still saying it Ben did it. 'Boom', he shot a hole through the wall into the latch from outside of the room. He pulled the door open before Jason could finish his sentence.

After entering the brightly lit room they both stood just inside the doorway mesmerized by what came into view. Neither man could manage to break the silence. How could anything top what they had seen in the last room with the fat mummy. After a few moments Jason was nearly in tears when he blurted out a few words.

"My God Benjamin," he solemnly said. "I keep repeating this same statement, this son-of-a-bitch is sicker than anyone's imagination could possibly allow. They're all just babies attached to a rigged up life support system. They're all taped and bound. Ben, they can't even move. They're helpless and at his mercy to do whatever he chooses. There must be at least seven of them."

"Let's just get out of here. There is nothing else we can do here but fester with hatred. Let's just go outside and wait for him to come back. God willing we can put him in hell where he belongs. And then, we can see if we can get someone out here to help the infants"

"Look over here Benjamin, the whole area outside is under surveillance; from the gate to the house, and inside of the house, this monitor here shows even the inside of the ambulance. That bastard was watching us all of the time."

"I don't think so... I think he just came inside to worship. I don't think he seen us or he would have probably came out of here shooting to protect his domain. I don't believe he looked in here on the children. After all they can't go anywhere. They're just being cultivated for him and his monster next door."

Jason had turned back around facing the children.

"They're all less than a year old. I don't know what anybody could do to help them other than to unplug the life support system. What do you think?"

"I said... I don't know!" Ben yelled.

"I don't... know what to do. The only thing I can think of is to help them kill that son-of-a-bitch that placed them in here like this in the first place."

"Do you think we should unplug everything in here or not Benjamin?"

"Can't you hear me Jason," Ben shouted. "I keep telling you that I don't know what we should do."

"The statement that, 'they're still alive' in this case, means that they are not completely dead. There is no mother. There are no voices to hear, no one can touch them through the glass incubators lids. There's no movement in their eyes. What has our God let occur here?"

"I... don't... know... I don't know is all that I'm willing to say. I'm hoping this is one of my worst nightmares and I'll awaken and these children will be playing with rattles and laughing at whatever makes babies laugh. I'm just a man Jason. I'm not capable of understanding sick men with sick faiths that justify committing sick acts that inflict pain upon others. You may have been right when you said 'to kill him will not kill the beast that has conquered mankind's inner soul for centuries upon centuries.' These kinds of acts are justified in the minds of those that are trying to please one god or another at the expense of others."

"Yea well... I know for sure that God never dreamed that mankind could be so wicked, even with the help of an evil spirit, if there is such a thing. So, I'm saying to you that I don't know either, but I do know that this has nothing to do with the wishes of God. This kind of ruthlessness comes from the wayward evil that dwells deep inside the minds of men and it grows like cancer. It has no path to follow but it does have the glory of surviving with self-praise and sexual satisfaction as a meaningful reward. This notion that anyone can be mightier than the Love of God through the crying voices of children, needs to be stomped out by men like us, and not ever forgiven by mankind.

So... how are we going to kill this thing when it gets back? How can we lock his spirit to the death of his body? How can we encapsulate his every thought and memory along with his lifeless body and cast them into hell so it won't spread from asshole to asshole on earth any longer?" asked Jason.

"Hey... I keep telling you, listen to me please. I'm not trying to analyze it; I'm going to just kill it."

"But you do know that if we can get him to kill himself it supposedly kills his spirit's ability to move on into another or into the idle minds of other self-centered men."

"No Jason, I don't even know that. I'm sworn to protect citizens of our community especially the children and obviously I am failing. All I know is I want to satisfy my own need to destroy those evil sacks of shit."

The two men went back outside and leaned side by side against body of the truck. Ben leaned forward and made noises as if he was going to vomit on the ground in front of him. He held it in and stood back up right. The anger within was very visual upon his face. He checked and made sure that both of his weapons had full clips, Jason did the same. They were both over whelmed with the obsession and the desire to kill. Ben obviously heard a sound and suddenly gazed out onto the horizon and started to move quickly towards the gate with Jason running right beside him.

"What do you see," ask Jason.

"There's a car coming," he said, "this has got to be our man."

Without taking his eyes off of the horizon he moved faster than Jason had ever seen the big man step without actually running.

It was starting to get dark and the oncoming car would soon have to have its lights turned on in order to be able to navigate the country road leading up to the gate. Either way daylight or dark the two of them intended to destroy the Locust killer on this night.

They both made it to the gate as the oncoming car was still slowly coming and still a good distance away. Ben grabbed his duffle bag he had hidden near the gate earlier and pulled out his 223 scoped rifle and handed to Jason as the car came closer to a point of just more than about two hundred yards. Ben and Jason both crotched down on the brim of the corn field out of site but within a few leaps from the gate. They patiently waited for the child killer to arrive.

"When he gets up to the gate we'll give him what he deserves in a big explosive way. If we're lucky our bullets won't take their toll too quickly. I want him to die slow enough for us to take pride in our kill."

"I'm ready" said Ben. I'm still a little apprehensive about committing a murder by ambush in the fashion of a coward but this is one time I'll make allowance.

Did you see that? He just turned on the headlights. He's driving awfully slow, I hope he doesn't suspect anything. We would never make it all the way back to our car in time to catch him if he turns around and leaves," Ben said.

"Actually Benjamin, it's too late for him to get away," Jason whispered as if it were possible for him to be heard at that distance. "I want him dead so bad that I think I could and probably should take my best shot right this moment and hit him from here, especially if he gets another fifty yards closer. Do you think I should take the shot and kill him right now or wait until he is closer?"

"Actually you're the marksman I know you could hit him from here with ease." Jason raised up a little and asked Ben if he would like him to take the shot and make the kill right now.

"No, let's just wait, I need to be a part of this kill no matter what the consequences. He's still coming, a lot slower now, but still coming our way. If he turns around at this point you take the shot while I run at him shooting before he can get turned around if you should miss, that way we can make sure he doesn't escape," said Ben.

"No doubt, but if we can, let's just let him come and climb right onto our lap. It's better this way. I want to be able to see and hear the impact of each shot fired."

"We can almost count the seconds now. He's driving a little faster now. I knew you and I wouldn't give him the option of killing himself, but rather than messing up a nice car let's let him step out for the surprise of his life," said Jason.

"I'll surprise myself if I can manage to let the car come to a complete stop."

Ben put down pulled out his hand gun. The car finally pulled up to the gate. The door opened slightly and the inside lights came on just as Ben anxiously fired two shots through the driver's side open window. In one swift move he grabbed the door handle, yanked it all the way open and roughly dragged the person out of the vehicle and down onto the ground.

"Wait, wait please don't hurt me!" a female voice screamed as both men had driven their guns against her body and ready to continue firing before they realized... it was Helen. "Helen!" Jason yelled, "My God baby, what are you doing here? Whose car is this? You nearly got yourself killed. Why... are... you here honey?" he asked, while shaking his hand in her face and yet not giving her a chance to answer.

Ben put his guns back in its place and remarked,

"Are you hurt? Did I hit you! Holly shit, I can't believe this. I nearly killed you."

"Are you guy's crazy? Thank goodness I'm not dead. I don't believe I'm hit; I just have glass all over me and two big holes in my friend's dashboard. What are you guys doing? You could have killed me. Jason what are you doing shooting up my friend's car?"

"Okay, okay honey I'm sorry, so sorry honey. We thought you were the child killer. Again, I now calmly ask... what are you doing here?"

"I'm sorry. I wanted to warn you and show you what I found, but every time I called the phone just gave me a busy signal. So, I used my friend's car that has a gps to find my way here. Now I'm the one that's sorry. I never dreamed you two could act so recklessly. I was just trying to help and make sure you knew what you were up against."

"We've got to get this car out of sight. It's too late to try and get you back down the road without a chance that he'll be passing you and getting suspicious. Let's get it out of sight over in the high corn over there," he said as he pointed.

Ben drove the car deep into the corn and completely out of sight. When he returned Jason and Helen were embraced and talking softly between hugs.

"What now," Ben asked. "We can't back down on our plan now so we'll have to change it a little so we don't kill the wrong person. We've still got to get this son-of-a- bitch, but obviously we've got to make sure that it's him. We almost messed up big time."

"Listen to me," Helen said as she broke away from Jason's arms.

"I was waiting for Jason to return since early this morning. He had said he would only be gone for a few hours. When it got later than six I couldn't stand it anymore. I wanted to be at the side of my man once I realized the grave danger that you guys were in. I called and called."

"We couldn't get a signal where we were."

"I know that now. But I need to let you know that this man you are trying to catch has killed more than children. He's the same man that has murdered as many as seven children fourteen years ago up in Erie. According to the newspaper article I found, he also broke the necks of two grown men when they attempted to hold him for the police. It made mention that he had actually snapped their necks with unexplained strength. The two men had stumbled across him in his attempt to bury the children's bodies. Back then the police believed that he was a part of a cult that worships that god named Molech that demanded that people sacrifice virgin children. I came to take my Jason home before he gets into something that's bigger than him and you put together. Please both of you, let's just get out of here and let the police handle his capture and punishment before the two of you either get hurt or killed."

"It's too late now, there's a car speeding up the road way. This one is not hesitating; he knows where he's going without a doubt. Jason, un-jam the gate and let's get back to the house to welcome him home. Helen please go and get into your friend's car and don't start it to leave until you see him reach the house and turn off his car lights. We'll flick the lights on and off on his car when it's safe for you to get out of here. Jason and I will see you later back in Pittsburgh, this I promise you. He's coming awfully fast Jason, we've got 'to get moving.

"Honey please, I'm scared of this man. Please come home with me and let Ben handle that man and his god. Please, please, please."

"I love you babe. I'll be alright. I'll see you when I get home in couple of hours. This is no god. This is just a child murdering psycho that needs to be stopped on this day. Get going, remember don't start your car until you see the signal like Ben said. Then you drive home as fast as you can. I'll see you there later I promise."

Chapter Twenty One

"Let's move Jason we only have a few minutes to get set up."

With-in minutes, the Land Rover reached the gate and this time he opened and closed it behind him. He sped for the house and pulled up directly in front of the ambulance truck. He left the lights of the car on to enable him to see and open the secret entry. Just as he turned back towards his car lights Ben and Jason rushed him catching him by surprise. They struggle for a moment while throwing him to the ground and cuffing him. "What are you people doing on my property?" He calmly asked. "I have no money but you can have the car and the laptop lying on the front seat. You can take it and I won't call the police, I swear."

"Shut up." Ben demanded.

Jason, click the car lights on and off to signal Helen to leave.

They watched as her lights came on and she slowly began to move.

"Cut the bullshit buddy we're not here to rob you. We're here to show you the rewards for sick and evil acts against babies," said Ben.

"I don't know what you're talking about. I'm a physician and this is my home."

"I thought I told you to shut up! Open the ambulance door Jason so we can reintroduce the fine doctor to his waiting patients. Oh yea and wait until you see what we've done to your big fat friend."

The doctor stopped talking and willingly entered into the grill of the truck.

After walking through the tunnel over the buggy tracks the three men reached the main junction and the two entryways. Ben shoved the cuffed man down onto the ground in front of Molech's worship chamber door first.

"Welcome the fuck home doc," said Jason.

Ben raised him a little and dragged him through the doorway into the room that housed Molech.

"There's your god," he said after clicking on the light switch.

To their surprise Molech was not the way they had left him. It was spine chilling for both men to see that the mummified fat man was no long slumped down like they had left him. He was now sitting back upright in his resting place. The bullet holes were still visible but there he sat with an eerie smile upon his face. He was no longer bleeding the black blood.

Jason immediately pulled out Bet-Lou and frantically fired into the corpse just as before. The impact of the bullets kicked it backwards against mountain dirt wall behind him, just as before. "This shit is super strange," Ben said as he shoved the cuffed doctor up near the pit that had been dug just in front of the shot-up mummy. "This is the second time old fat boy here has been riddled with lead. He still keeps looking alive."

"What have you fools done? This is America; you idiots can't interfere with my right to worship. I have a constitutional right to worship whom I please, when and where I please."

"I thought I told you to shut the fuck up before I put a bullet in your head. You have the same rights as the children in the next room," Ben said to him. "I just stopped in here to give you a chance to say goodbye to your child killing god. Obviously you've rigged him up some how to retract and sit back up."

Ben let go of his grip on the doctor and pointed his pistol at Molech and fired again just for the hell of it. "How many shots can your dead god take doc.? He doesn't seem to want to leave you just yet."

Following Ben's lead, Jason put two more shots into the plump belly of the beast this time exposing what appeared to be a chewed-up child's hand with fingers still attached.

The doctor had gotten down on his knees with his forehead pressed against the ground. He was chanting in a language that was unknown to both Jason and Ben. Suddenly he finished his prayer in English. Without warning he loudly yelled,

"I do this in the name of you my father and a hundred fathers before you. That we may someday win your favor, and accordingly we shall live as those that have eaten from the tree of everlasting life."

"That's enough of this bullshit doc. Your fat friend has been dead for at least a thousand years. The only thing that keeps him alive now is you and your evil ways and… guess what doc? It all ends on this day."

Just as Jason ended his sentence he heard Helen scream.

"My God, oh my God Jason, what's going on?"

"Not again," Ben said as Jason ran from the worship room where he was and into the room next door where the children were located and he embraced Helen as she stood in the doorway.

"Baby, listen to me. What are you doing back here? I asked you to go home. Why are you still here?"

They had moved slightly into the room that held the seven children. "All of these babies." She was crying between words. "Jason, look at them, all these helpless babies. Please Jason, let this be one of your nightmares… Look Jason, they are all reaching out for me at the same time. Jason, they want their mothers. Let's get them out of here right now."

"Why didn't you just leave honey," he asked, while holding her tightly against his chest and ignoring her comment.

"The car was stuck," she said sobbingly, "and I couldn't get it out of the field… Oh Jason look at them."

"Okay baby, listen to me; all of this evil is about to come to an end. This beast has committed his last murder."

"But… What about the children Jason? They're being kept alive like babies on life support. We've got to do something for them Jason."

"I know, I know."

Just then Ben came into the room dragging the cuffed Doctor along behind him.

"Now what Jason, we've got to wrap this up. Take Helen out of here and I won't be far behind the two of you. I'm going to do it myself."

"No," you" can't let Ben kill them this way Jason," Helen said as she looked straight into Jason's eyes. "Remember you told me that no one can kill the spirit of an evil man that has been cursed. You said that the evilness will simply move to another that's present. What if it moves into you or Ben, or even into me, then what?"

The Doctor smiled at the thought and knew that she was right.

He knew that his Molech would continue his glorious quest for a perfect world of his own in spite of the wishes of a coming world of love and harmony as depicted by the Holy Bible. His world with the holly sacrifice of the innocent gave him what he wanted and needed to be just as God. He thought that's where he would live on in spirit forever, even if he were put to death. He knew inside that he had brought many children to his god as sacrifices and that he would not be forsaken.

"I don't care," said Ben; "this one is going to die at my hands. There is no boogie-man. He and he alone is the one that has killed again and again without mercy. He's the one that sat up this big fat corpse and praises something dead while he kills in its name. When this one dies all of his threats will die with him."

Ben lifted the Doctor up against the wall and 'pow', shot him in his left leg at point blank. The doctor moaned and painfully fell to the ground.

"No Benjamin! Helen may just very well be right"

"More bullshit Jason; you and I both know that this is just a man that has been able to instill fear by committing horrific crimes and happens to be a child murdering psychopath. That bull shit about him being some self-proclaimed blood line for thousands of years, of a god that survives by the sacrificial deaths of children is part of his own sickness."

"Okay, but can we just listen to what she has to say. What can it hurt to just hear her through?"

Helen was hysterically frightened by the sight of the children and now the sight of the doctor bleeding from Ben's gunshot wound. The babies were all crying, squirming and arching their backs as if attempting to break free. Their eyes were wide open with an expression of helplessness and yet anger. Each child was inside of an incubator that was attached to a homemade life support apparatuses that had a metal cable that locked them to their own cribs. They appeared to all be less than one year old. Their bodies were extremely under-developed and their appearance looked more like oversized embryos than early aged infants. They were being treated like livestock that's being fattened for a harvest. Each one was totally captive and was going to be kept alive for at least another six years; and they all gave off an eerie sense of knowing their fate.

Helen noticed that there were at least another twenty empty glass incubators waiting to be filled. Now she too was exploding inside, for the moment she too wanted revenge just as Jason and Ben. She momentarily calmed herself down. She was doing her best to stay focused and keep looking at a bigger picture in her own feminist mind. She spoke up in an attempt to stay calm instead of her true feeling of wanting to see this man dead just as the two of them.

"Jason, wasn't it you that told me that 'this kind of evil cannot be killed'. You said that 'the only way to end the reign of a curse is to end the blood line of the fools that have worshiped and carried it forward for years and maybe even centuries'."

"Yes honey, I did say just that, but we are not going to let this man walk out of here and kill again. His life as we know it, as well as the threat of killing, must be taken away and this is his night and we are the chosen men to do it. If not, we might as well let him kill us, as cowards, right here and now on this spot."

"Not this one, why doesn't anyone ever hear me. I said... he will kill no more," Ben said, as he fired another bullet into the other leg of the Doctor.

The second loud bang of Ben's weapon momentarily startled Helen again, but she bravely continued her plea.

"Look Ben, can't you see that he is no ordinary man. He's just lying there smiling at you. He's not harmed by the tearing of his flesh. We've got to do something different to end the life of a man that's capable of doing this type of thing to children. That's all I'm saying. The kind of evil that's going on here is unstoppable. From what Jason has said, to kill him is like trying to kill a tree by trimming off its dead branches; it will grow faster and stronger."

"Don't worry; from what I've experienced as a police officer all these years, he will be dead and gone. There will be no smile on his face or any more babies' blood on his hands. He is sacrificing his own life to the fat dead god in the next room, he just wants me to help, don't you doc. Go head tell her that you want to die for your god," he commented while giving the doctor a chance to agree with a head nod.

"Honey," Jason said, "how do you think we can convince this crazy man to take his own life? Look at him. He and his god has been self-glorified and praised for years based upon his makeup of being a man that saves lives as a pediatrician. He has been stealing lives out of the wombs of mothers by convincing them that their babies had died before birth and then bringing them here to sacrifice them like dead animals. Some of the children were even rejected as not being clean enough.

"I agree with you and Ben but let's be fair about this for the sake of argument. He's already bleeding and he can't heal himself; tell him to let Molech heal him right now right in front of us. Tell him to let Molech save him from Ben's next bullet. Tell him to let Molech cause him to rise up and break the cuffs that bind him. Let him tell his Molech to give him the strength to cast the three of us into the lap of his god, instead of those small helpless babies. Let's challenge him to use the power of his god against our determination to kill him right in the sight of his prey. Go ahead Jason tell him. If he sees that he cannot, maybe he will give up and jump into his own fire to prove himself."

"Okay Helen," said Jason," you've made the challenge, now rather than firing the killing shot and he live again, we'll give him the count of ten for him to call on his god as his savior to show him what a fool he has been. The curse that is responsible for evil fools like him must cease to exist. Put him at the feet of his god to burn as his own sacrifice. Let's see if the mighty subject of Molech can bring him away from the same fires that he has cast so many stolen lives of so many children."

"You both might have a point," said Ben while smiling in the face of the bleeding Doctor. He was no longer smiling but looking as if he were beginning to think. The doctor mustered up one more smile that quickly turned to a very loud laugh before saying;

"So... why didn't your God save the thousands of children that have been thrown into the pits of sacrifice to my god? Why didn't He bring them out of the fire? Wasn't it He who directed the sacrifice of men and beast as a pleasing aroma of flesh and the taking of lives that He Himself had created? Where was He when my father's father and his fathers before him took the worthless lives of the many first born sons or the many daughters that were unfortunate enough to be born before a male child? I'm laughing now because as the big fool that you say I am and fathers were, you and yours must often wonder why your God has managed to turn His eyes away from our so called evil folly, for even to this day and while we speak millions of your children have died while in prayer to no avail and have died at our hands.

Of course I'm laughing now. Wouldn't you if you knew like I know that none of you will leave this hole in this mountain alive, but I will. Those squirming and reaching hands of these now defiled children; will end up in lap of Molech in spite of your gallant efforts. Of course

I'm laughing. Maybe the three of you should commit suicide rather than let Molech digest your blood while it runs warm through your veins. Look at my wounds; they no longer bleed. Go in and look at my god; you will see that he too has stopped the bleeding again. At this very moment he is anxiously waiting to devour you and all your blessings and the succulent taste of your non-virgin flesh and blood. Yes I'm laughing but why aren't you? Here... this is what I do to your chains that bind me."

He stood up and snapped the handcuffs as if they were made of pretzels. The ground beneath vibrated and shook from the activities in the next room. The children were now crying out-loud in panic as Helen, Ben and Jason looked on in startled amazement.

"Where is your bravery now Mr. Ben? What about your bitch Mr. Jason, or are you really Oz? Why is she now so silent and shivering?"

The doctor took his right hand and put it between the legs of Helen and then lifted her off the ground and back against the wall.

"How does that feel bitch? Do you think it feels good enough to make me want to commit suicide for you," he said as his eyes turned as red as fire, "huh, do you like it, huh?"

As if suddenly awakening Jason leaped on the back of the doctor, he wrapped his left forearm around the his neck and applied all of his strength in and attempt to choke him to death while pushing Bet-Lou against his rib cage and firing two shots. The doctor quickly turned around and elbowed Jason under his right jaw bone and broke free of Jason's grip. Even though he was shot he managed to toss Jason to the floor like a rag doll. He administered two swift kicks to Jason's head knocking him out cold.

Being careful not to hit Jason or Helen, Ben also took two shots into the doctor while he was standing over Jason. The doctor turned and grabbed Ben in one sweeping motion and threw him down onto the floor beside Jason and at the feet of Helen who now stood alone there in total shock. He straddled over both men and looked deep into at their faces with a puzzled look, he roared.

"I see the blackened eyes of two wayward angels in both of your faces. None the less, you will both still serve as tributes to my god of gods."

Helen dropped down to her knees next to Jason and lifted him into her arms.

"Baby, baby," she repeated again and again, "please get Oz to get us out of here."

"So," the doctor roared loudly as if he finally felt the pain caused by the bullets that were lodged in his chest, "you are Oz the great revenger. Well it doesn't matter down here; in this hell you have no connection to your God Mr. Oz."

He then looked to Ben.

"You know what Mr. Ben or are you Esha? I think I'll take you into my father's den first. I'm sure he'll make allowance for your age and, who really knows, you may still be a virgin of sort, like the full grown virgins that died as the sacrifices of my counterpart Jim Jones and his followers. My, what a glorious day that was. More than nine hundred souls willingly sacrificed in just one of your days"

He struck Ben on the side of his face to insure that he would not be strong enough to resist. He grabbed him by both of his ankles and dragged him out of that room and into the sacrifice den of his great Molech.

After a few moments Helen could hear the doctor chanting loudly at the top of his voice. She was sobbing and grasping for air along with the seven captive babies that were still bound by their incubators.

"Please honey wake up."

She stood up and grabbed Jason by his shirt and began to drag him out towards the tunnel leading back to the house just as the doctor returned. He shoved her to the ground as he rushed pass her and began to break the glass of the incubators. He began lifting out the children. He grabbed three of them at a time and headed on his way back to the other room.

After about fifteen minutes of dragging Jason without stopping, she reached the ambulance with Jason still knocked out cold. She was scuffling to get him up into the cab of the truck when he suddenly began to stir.

His eyes were wide open and had change from brown to jet black. He stood up and momentarily became rigid and began to turn his head from side to side. With the loud voice of Oz he spoke out, "Where is Esha?" He flexed his quickly changing muscular body to a point where Helen did not recognize his body structure as being that of Jason's. Jason was now massive and muscular along with being quick thinking and alert to his surroundings.

"I feel the pain of my friend. Where is Esha I asked you?" Helen did not answer; she just pointed down into the mine shaft. He immediately climbed back down into the tunnel and without another word ran into the darkness away from Helen.

"You get him Oz," she whispered to herself, "you kill those bastards, him and his god for what they've done to the children, you get'm Jason." She repeated as she had had enough. With those last words upon her lips she closed her eyes and passed out from exhaustion.

Jason had taken on his angelic form as Oz and Oz was as furious as any being could possibly get about the slaughter of the children and now the fact that his fellow angel's life was in jeopardy.

Chapter Twenty Two

'They built high places in the valley of Ben Hinnon
to sacrifice their sons and daughters to Molech, though I
never command nor did it enter my mind that they could
do such detestable things' GOD... Jeremiah 32:35

When Jason reached the junction he realized that he was deep into the mountain side and that there was no longer the life supporting light and darkness of the world outside that he needed in order to be connected to his angelic lifeline. It was pitch black except for the reflection of light from the fire coming from around and beneath the metal door. He found himself weakening as he got further away from Helen and the world outside of this hell hole. He realized that he was losing the driving spirit of Oz and taking back the humanness of Jason. He could hear the evil growl of the doctor and the loud panting of Molech. The screaming sounds of the children were becoming clear as he got closer. Jason, out of breath, knelt down on one knee. He had completely reverting back to himself. Without the Godly strength of Oz he knew that he was going to be back in trouble very soon.

Barely strong enough to stand, he made it up to the door and grabbed George from his other holster and pushed the door open. Ben was necked and strapped down between the now wide open legs of Molech with his face buried in his lap just below his huge stomach.

The dead god, still riddled with healed bullet holes, had his blood red eyes wide open. The fire in the pit was blazing hot and about to be fed with another screaming child that the doctor was holding above his head while chanting in a garbled language. The eyes of the god were opening and slowly closing with a facial expression of being satisfied with bliss with one of God's angels in his lap and the last of the seven children being sacrificed into the fire.

Jason was becoming incoherent but still managed to fire his weapon with accuracy into the back of the doctor five times, knocking him forward into the fiery pit with the child in his hands. The doctor screamed as he fell into the pit because of imbalance due to the slight weight of the infant. It wasn't the gun shots that took him into the pit, it was the child. The flames swirled as if trying to spit back the nasty taste of the evil spirit of the doctor to no avail. Under the mental command of Molech, Ben turned and reached out in an attempt to rescue and pull the doctor back out of the flames. Jason was motionless for split second as Ben loudly screamed out Jason's names while leaping from the lap of Molech over the flames and knocking Jason to the ground. His eyes were changed from his own to the pure redness of the beast that sat above them.

"No!" Jason yelled out to Ben, "It's me Benjamin. It's, Jason."

Ben with the intruding force of Molech stood above Jason. Molech was well in control of Ben's mind. He snatched Jason up as to throw him into the fire which now held the burning and screaming body of the doctor. Both Jason and Helen, who had miraculously made her way back to the room, were calling out to Ben. Somehow their voices seemed to reach him as he dropped Jason back to the ground and paused while looking strangely and directly into Jason's brown eyes. He reached down and grabbed Jason's weapon and placed it against Jason's head. Helen was standing on the other side of the pit screaming relentlessly.

"No Ben please, don't kill him. In the name Ehsa and the love of God, I beg of you."

Ben looked over at Helen with his eyes now flashing back and forth from black to red. Suddenly with his eyes paused as Esha and fully black, he turned around and unloaded the weapon into the belly of Molech. While the god was stunned by the unexpected change of events, Esha leaped back across the burning pit into the fat chest of the beast. Esha instantly transformed back into Ben and with-in a split second Ben took one last looked at Jason and Helen. He slightly smiled and with all of his human might he pulled Molech down on top of himself and into the burning pit. The fire acted as if it had been ignited with gasoline, it flamed high into the ceiling and swallowed up the doctor, Ben, the child and Molech. The quick explosive flash of fire quickly extinguished itself in a matter of seconds except for the ceiling above, which was made of black coal. It seemed to burst into flames with a fire of its own.

"Run Helen run! Let's get out of here. Don't worry about me, I'm right behind you. Just run!"

They ran with the ceiling flames breathing down their necks. From the door of Molech up through the tunnel they ran until they reached the ambulance and made their exit back into the world above.

Finally outside Jason again began to transform into Oz. He stopped in his tracks and pushed Helen away while telling her to go on without him.

While looking back into the cave he shouted, "Esha where are you my friend?"

He watched as the flames made their way up through the mine shaft and began to swallow up the truck like it were a huge match and quickly spread and engulfed the attached house. He attempted to go back into the ambulance entryway but Helen had clamped herself around his ankles and was pleading with him not to go back into the fire.

"I must perish with my comrade of eternity. Without him there is no Oz there is no Jason. Speak to me Esha what must I do to find you?"

"No! Jason please, one sacrifice is enough in exchange for the death of this Molech and all of his followers. To sacrifice another would give glory to those that hate what God stands for. Right this moment all those that believe and take part in his evilness will perish with their god. Please, you stay here with me or drag me in with you. I will not live without you and I will not let go. Jason I love you," she shouted above the noise of the now roaring flames.

Oz struggled momentarily in an attempt to free himself from Helen without harming her. She held fast with all of her might. Oz took a few steps towards the flames but could not break free of her grasp.

Oz paused with his eyes focused on movement with-in the burning flames he spoke into the fire as if talking to his comrade.

"I hear you my brother! Release him and come out from the flames or I shall come in and stand beside you." Within a few seconds the fire lit up the base of the mountain as well as some of the corn field around the entryway. Helen was still holding onto her man for dear life.

"God," she said, "please don't let him go in."

Ben's warm and manly voice came from the flames so that even Helen could hear.

"I've got this one brother. I'm going to hold him until this one is no more, now or ever to come. You go home my friend and complete our task for his reflections and blind followers are still among you. I will always be right there by your side."

Jason began to slowly back away with Helen yet at his feet and pulling him towards a safe distance. The force of the fire was pushing at their faces. They slowly moved further and further away before giving in to exhaustion from their final fight with Molech. As they lie on the ground at a safe distance Helen curled up into the arms of Jason with her back against his chest and facing the fire. Both Jason and Helen's eyes were on the flames waiting, hoping and expecting that Esha would somehow emerge and bring Ben back from certain death. Tears formed in the solid black eyes of Oz as he began to realize that Ben has made the ultimate sacrifice to save him and the many children still out the world that may be held captive in the homes of the sick and the selfish by a curse and a god that could not die in any other way.

Finally giving up and leaning back Helen, and now Jason, were both greeted by the innocence of the star lit night sky above while the fire continued to rage and consumed what was left of the worship chamber of Molech.

After a short while of silence Helen whispered a question to Jason.

"Honey, right now, you are Jason, right?"

"Yes."

"Are you the man Jason or Jason the angel Oz?"

"I'm the man Jason that loves you," he calmly answered.

She paused for a while appearing to be in deep thought.

She pulled herself away from the secure feeling of Jason's chest and turned around facing him and looked him directly into his now brown eyes surround by the normal white of a human.

"Are you sure you are Jason," she asked, signifying some level of doubt.

"Yes I am, but I know I may have just lost a friend.

I don't know if or how he could have, or even that he wanted to survive that fiery pit. If he did not survive it means that he just made the ultimate sacrifice to save the both of us and maybe many more to come. The thought that I may never see his face or have the confidence of knowing that there may not be another man anywhere that would kill to protect us. All of these thoughts are upon me. I hurt inside, I miss him already and I need to hear his voice for the comfort in knowing that we've done the right thing."

"Yes… you are truly my Jason. Can my Jason please take me home now?"

THE END

Excerpts

"It's not just an eye for an eye. A child's life has no equal. One tear of a child should be a fair exchanged for the life of a predator, especially when it comes to sexual violence committed upon an innocent child. I believe they are all innocent! They are here by the grace of God and the pride of His achievements. The very first commandment 'To be fruitful and multiply,' was not for the sake of the lustful hunger within those that are obviously sick and evil!"

~

One dim light revealed a spine tingling sight. It was that of a huge mummified man clad in bronze like metal from the bottom of his rib cage up to his neck. He was sitting with his legs wide open and the heels of his feet resting on what appeared to be a sacrifice pit. His belly was much larger than the rest of his body and very much out of proportion. The bottom of the pit was filled with slightly glowing ashes. Above the pit high against the wall was a camera facing the mummified man. Jason found himself tingling with uneasiness as he quickly began backing out of the room while nervously attempting to call Ben on his cell phone. The phone lit up but there was no signal. The mummy's eyes appeared to turn his way as he grunted out a low pitch noise.

~

"We've got to do something different to end the life of a man that's capable of doing this type of thing to children. That's all I'm saying. The kind of evil that's going on here is unstoppable. From what Jason has said, to kill him is like trying to kill a tree by trimming off its dead branches; it will grow faster and stronger."